BITTEN BY TIME

LARA BRONSON

Tacit Press, LLC

BITTEN BY TIME

BITTEN BY TIME

To my readers

BITTEN BY TIME

"Do you believe in destiny? That even the powers of time can be altered for a single purpose? That the luckiest man who walks on this earth is the one who finds… true love?"

—DRACULA, BRAM STOKER

CHAPTER 1

"*You're never more aware of your surroundings than when you plan on traveling to a new corner of the world.*" The thought brought me back to the Sea-Tac airport café, where I was waiting for my friend and roommate Mei to get us some coffee. Since the numbers on the clock neared two a.m., everything seemed a bit slower than usual, as if time or the perception of it resembled a disoriented sleepwalker's steps. The barista, in a daze, kept moving the same cup from one place to another, a neighboring coffee drinker missed the sipping hole repetitively, and another traveler gave up entirely as he collapsed in the middle of an airport path. Yes, everyone felt the pressure of sleeplessness—everyone except Mei.

When Mei approached the barista and squeaked her hello, it startled him out of his slumber. She then gave a glorious smile, making him blush though still in a daze, till he heard her order: "I'd like a Venti latte with one vanilla, two pumps of caramel syrup, three pumps of mocha, one pump of raspberry, double blended, with low fat whipped cream, caramel, and mocha drizzle." Mei knew her favorite recipe so well that she could recite it like an incantation.

She turned toward me and mouthed: "What do you want?"

I answered in the same mime style, "an Americano, please. Thank you." I didn't want to torment the poor guy even more. He had had enough with one exuberant UW student.

When the barista received my order request, the relief lowered his shoulders. But that's how Mei was. Her jovial enthusiasm knew no limit, especially since her best friend, aka me, planned on traveling across the ocean to her dream destination. Since Mei and I were roommates at the University of Washington campus, she knew more about me than I learned about myself. So, when she heard I finally took the plunge and bought tickets to Romania, she jumped up and down in excitement.

For some, Romania didn't seem like a dream destination, but given that my father was Romanian and my Bachelor's degree was in History, the trip's significance became apparent. When my dad heard the news, he couldn't contain his tears as if his daughter planned to become the first solo woman to embark on some kind of ancestral archeological exploration. But let's be honest, everything they could find on those lands had already been discovered. Nonetheless, Mom had to calm him numerous times until she provided one of her "rejuvenating" teas, and suddenly he got better.

They didn't think much of the reason behind my decision, considering it a graduation present. But there was a second reason why I chose to leave for a while.

It happened when I least expected it. He was my boyfriend at the time, the one who finally stuck. All prior dates ghosted me like shadows in the night right after our first date, as if something about me spooked them, so they never returned to ask for a second date. But not Elijah. He stayed with me even during finals or when I had a fight with my mom about not coming home for Spring break. We had been dating for several months, and all was so dream-like, but he came on to me one night after a drunken party. I refused to sleep with him because I still wasn't ready. He tried to force himself on me. He ripped the buttons off my flannel shirt and scratched me while trying to remove my bra. I hit back hard, to the point where he was too drunk to fight, and I was too fired up to stop. I continued to slap him, which proved less effective. Kicking him in the shins produced far greater results. Afterward, he fell to the side, and I could finally breathe freely as his body weight had been lifted. He lay there half-asleep, defenseless, and I knew this was my only opportunity to take control of what had happened to me. I hit him a few more times as if he were a pillow, releasing all the anger, fear, and disappointment. The following day, I texted him to never look for me again and forget we were ever a thing.

He listened and never contacted me for a while, but then started stalking me. Several times, I felt a shadow lurking behind me. Sometimes it seemed like my imagination was at work. Other times, I could distinctly hear footsteps. So, I took control of the situation again, and I bought tickets to Romania the following week. I had never felt as strong before. I always feared the consequences of my actions, except when it came to Elijah.

Suddenly, the airport voice spoke, "*Ladies and gentlemen, flight 76D to Frankfurt will be delayed for another hour. Excuse the inconvenience. We appreciate your patience. Thank you.*"

Just when I decided to embark on the journey of my life, my flight got delayed for more than eight hours. The delay wasn't because of a big storm ravishing the land or unexpected high winds blasting the windows. No, just human error, which no one wished to divulge through the speakers. Everyone reacted to the news the same way, with a plenitude of disappointment.

For a second, I wished to return to my cozy bed filled with plushies and forget all this nonsense, but I couldn't. The trip meant too much, and this delay meant I was still stuck here with a past threatening to extend into my future. It was why I was leaving, so I could experience being me again in the surroundings of a different, new (to me) world. So I could learn to live without the hindrance of the memories of a failed relationship. I chose me, even when I wished to become nothing and simply disappear. Sometimes, I wondered how the world would continue to live without me. Will there be a blip of a difference? Most likely, not. The world would be fine and continue as usual. Good thing I didn't do it for the world or the pursuit of a perfect love story. I chose to face my life in its present form because it was the best, albeit the scariest, thing I could do. And now I was here taking the trip of my lifetime—number one on my bucket list.

"Earth to Petra. Please land safely. You aren't allowed to fly toward your dreams unless it's on a plane," said Mei while handing me my Americano. We both decided to match our outfits today, so we wore black leggings and a cropped top that said "Double" on mine and "Trouble" on hers.

"What can I do if fate delays my dream's fulfillment?" I said dejectedly.

"Hey, if not today, then tomorrow, but I will make sure to send you off on this trip of yours." She grinned.

"What do you mean today or tomorrow? It's already tomorrow. Look at the clock."

"You and your negative thinking." She teased.

"You meant to say realistic," I said and sipped some of my coffee.

"Better tell me what you are going to do in Romania. I don't mind hearing it again since I never quite listened the last bajillion times you told me," she said, smiling.

I wanted to protest her not-so-friend-like behavior, but it was late, and the situation had already aggravated me.

"Well, once I arrive in Brașov, I'll stay for a few nights in a hotel. I'll take my time and visit the city and then plan to travel to Bran Castle. Then, I'll–"

"Now that you're finally going to Transylvania, do you think you'll bump into Count Dracula?"

"How many times do I need to tell you? Vlad The Impaler, or Vlad Dracula, never lived or even visited Bran Castle. He ruled over Wallachia, a land next to Transylvania," I said, exasperated as Mei giggled like a schoolgirl.

"*This is the pre-boarding announcement for flight 76D to Frankfurt. We are now inviting passengers with small children and any passengers requiring special assistance to begin boarding. Please have your boarding pass and identification ready. Regular boarding will begin in approximately ten minutes. Thank you,*" said the airport voice.

"See, the sun hasn't come out yet," said Mei.

"As if the sun ever shines in the land of Seattle," I retorted.

"A drop of positivity never hurt anyone."

I hated when Mei was right. This time, I really wanted to listen to her advice. I was done with painful experiences tinting my happiness. My journey aimed at helping me heal and enjoy the pleasures of life the way I wanted to, not how others deemed it. I leaned on the back of the chair and exhaled deeply.

"You know I like to joke and stuff, but I'm happy you're going. The douchebag didn't deserve you. And when you pushed back, he retaliated by stalking you. Putting some distance between you and him will make a whole lot of a difference. And when you return to campus, you will have enough strength to move forward. Just know you didn't deserve it," Mei said as she held my hand and looked at me with her beautiful brown eyes.

I always knew how good of a friend Mei was. She never spoke of the incident before, always trying to protect my feelings, but now I could see it in her eyes the hatred we both shared for the man I once loved.

Mei sat beside me and enveloped one arm around my shoulders. We remained silent till it was my turn to embark on the plane. Mei came closer to me, hugged me, and said: "Listen, you've been working your butt off these past years to graduate top in your class. It's time to take a well-deserved vacation now that you're out of school. Take your time. Let loose. Vanish from this world for a bit. Enjoy the unknown for a while."

I was flabbergasted. Could Mei read my thoughts so

easily? “I am of the same opinion,” I said.

She then hugged me again and let me loose like a mother bird letting her chick spread its wings into the unknown vastness of the sky.

I threw my favorite knitted crossbody bag on my shoulder, grabbed the handle of my heavy yellow carry-on, all plastered with stickers of my favorite things, from coffee to the countries I still had to visit, and rushed to check-in. Mei kept waving, reluctant to separate. Though I couldn’t turn back yet, I was still mesmerized by what awaited me. But right before I stepped into the tunnel, I turned around and waved an exuberant goodbye, to which Mei responded in the same overly excited way.

As I entered the tunnel connecting me to my new adventure, I couldn’t help but question how my life would change after this journey of a lifetime.

CHAPTER 2

Upon arriving in Brașov, my body and mind reached complete exhaustion. An eleven-hour flight to Frankfurt, another two hours to Bucharest, and one hour to Brașov took a heavy toll on me. It boggled my mind how other travelers endured such torment repeatedly. At the beginning of my flight, I planned on sleeping the whole time. I even took a melatonin pill, but sleep refused to settle between my eyelids. The excitement woke me every time I closed my eyes. After several attempts, I gave up. During the entire trip to Europe, the flight attendants and I guarded all the peacefully sleeping and snoring men, women, kids, and even babies. One of the flight attendants took pity on me and offered a glass of liquor, but I refused. I didn't want to arrive in an unknown city tired AND tipsy. So, by the time the passengers exited the third plane, I was ready to collapse on the Romanian airport benches. Only by sheer will did I drag my feet to the luggage claim area, and by sheer will, I climbed into the first taxi willing to open its door for me.

Inside the cab, the driver, a man in his sixties wearing a flat cap, spoke cheerfully in a heavily accented English. His enthusiasm revigorated me and brought my attention to the scenery beyond the windows of his car. "*I am finally here,*" I thought.

"Where are you traveling from, miss?" the joyous taxi driver asked.

"I'm from the states. Washington state, to be precise," I said. Then I repeated the same phrase in Romanian to see his reaction.

"Oh, miss, you speak Romanian?" he interjected, turning toward me and almost losing control of the wheel.

"Is it such a rarity?" I asked.

"Oh, no. It's just I'm new to the taxi trade. I've been a professor my whole life. Since I retired, I missed having conversations with others, so I chose to drive people around. My wife always complains about the risks of getting mugged or beaten in this business, but I've only had wonderful experiences so far."

"I think it's a great opportunity to meet people this way. What did you teach?"

"I taught Romanian Mythology, miss. I held lectures in front of hundreds of students every week, and my wife still made me take out the trash." We both chuckled.

"We have similar professions. I studied History for my Bachelor, but for my Grad, I want to study something closer to my heart: 'The Evolution of Eastern European Linguistics.'"

"Why is it close to your heart, miss?" the driver asked.

"Well, my dad is Romanian. He and my mom met in Brașov and fell in love. They traveled the whole country together, and when it was time to leave, mom decided to stay here. My sister was born in Brașov as well, but when she turned two, they decided to move to Spokane, my mother's birthplace. I was born six years later."

"So Romanian blood flows through your veins, miss," he said.

"I guess." I wanted to stop talking about me and more about what he knew. "Could you tell me more about Romanian Mythology?"

"Oh, miss, I could tell you stories for weeks. I'm afraid a short drive would not be enough." His demeanor changed, resembling that of a professor.

"At least tell me a short summary, professor."

He chuckled to hide the flattery he felt.

"Fine, miss, you win. Romanian Mythology, like other European ones, stems from Greek or Roman deities but also from the core fears of humanity. Myths are quite valuable to our society as they represent a big part of our history and help us better understand the human mindset. Zburătorul, werewolves, and the most famous ones, *strigoii*, beings resembling vampires, represent the core of Romanian Mythology, each with their own genesis story and historical influence. Based on Stoker's novel, many have the impression that *strigoii* get their origins from Vlad the Impaler. But they have dwelled in the Romanian mentality for hundreds of years before."

"I know what I'm asking is pure rubbish, but I must. Was Vlad the Impaler the closest thing to a *strigoi*?" My face turned beet red, given how unprofessional the question was.

He laughed and said, "of course not. He remains one of the greatest rulers of our land, but he was never touched by magic."

I wished to ask more, potentially far more moronic but burning questions, but I feared divulging how much of a fan I was of Vlad the Impaler. It might've seemed like a stereotype, the half-Romanian girl fangirling over the cruelest Romanian ruler in history and the most infamous vampire in the world. But it bridged a bond with my sister. One we struggled to build for years. Finally, we could fangirl over someone together.

The first time Dad told my sister and me the story of how Vlad the Impaler fought an army far greater than his and how he punished the guilty in the cruelest of ways, my sister became obsessed. She would never stop talking about Vlad and his heroic deeds. And after months and months of blabbering, her curiosity spread to me. In an instant, Mom and Dad had two chatterboxes annoying their ears with Vlad the Impaler trivia. By the time she turned seventeen, my sister already knew she would study history at UW and, eventually, a master's degree in Eastern European Cultures. But she never got the chance to graduate.

I dismissed the thought and focused instead on the expert on Romanian Mythology and the inconsiderate number of questions roaming in my head. But, by the time I could formulate one, the car had arrived at the hotel. Dazed, I got out of the car as the driver carried my luggage to the doorsteps of the hotel. When I turned to ask his name, he was gone as if never there.

When I entered my hotel room in a semi-dormant state, I dropped my luggage to the side, threw myself on the cushiony bed, and went straight to sleep.

∞ ∞ ∞

Thirst woke me up in the middle of the night. For a moment, I forgot I had arrived in a new country, a new city, and in a new bed. A cool breeze caressed my cheeks. When I turned to the side, curious of where it came from, I noticed the window was open, and the white curtains fluttered under the air currents. "Weird, I don't remember opening the window last night," I said. When I went closer to it, I noticed the Brașovian houses gleaming from the full moon's light. It contrasted with the cold beam illuminating the giant Brașov sign on the mountain. It seemed like everyone was sleeping except me and the moon. As I pushed the window wider to inhale the freshness of the night's air, I noticed a strange fragrance emanating. I looked down from the third floor to check what could produce such a smell, but except for the asphalted roads, the worn-out clay tile roofs, and a few trees, there was nothing. My gaze went to the sides, and upon a closer look, I saw pots of flowers hanging from the adjacent window. "*It must be the flowers*," I thought. But flowers usually smelled sweet, while this aroma had earthy notes. Though a familiar scent, I had a hard time pinpointing its origin. In the end, the night's deep silence gave me some tranquility and compelled me to try and give sleep another shot.

Morning caught me lying with eyes wide open and glued to the ceiling. As if remaining motionless somehow would convince my brain to fall asleep. "Cursed be the jet lag," I said. By the time it reached six a.m., I was ready for coffee. Copious amounts of coffee. I didn't feel like dressing up, so I put on a simple T-shirt with space kittens, distressed jean shorts, and my not-so-white sneakers. When

I stepped out into the street, the crisp mountain air welcomed me, offering a much-needed rejuvenation. I walked for half a mile to the closest café from the hotel called The Coffee Tree. Brașov resembled Seattle in many ways but with an added old European flare, especially the burnt orange rooftops contrasting with the dewy fog of the mountains. Nothing about the houses I encountered resembled a cookie-cutter American home. The façade of the houses varied between bright colors of mint, blush pink, and yellow. Some had tall, ornate metal gates, while others had no gates at all. The roofs challenged one another with different forms, from pointy domes to office-like rectangles. You could feel the clash of new and old, and for the most part, history won.

At the coffee shop, the mood of the interior swung a hundred and eighty degrees, transposing me into an urban setting with chalk art on walls, wooden crates for benches, and pillows scattered everywhere. The menu written on a massive chalkboard spread from floor to ceiling also included cheerful messages from previous customers. It felt like a refuge from everything one might want to run away from, like troubles of the heart or ghosts of the past.

I took the warm paper cup from a handsome barista who recounted his own trip to Texas till my stomach growled at the most inopportune of moments. I hadn't had breakfast yet. He chuckled and recommended I try the bakery next door.

I didn't have the nerve to tell him I usually chose savory breakfasts. But then again, a croissant wouldn't hurt. "*I'm on vacation, for crying out loud,*" I thought. "*Might as well live a little.*"

Indeed, as the barista said, the bakery was several feet away from the coffee shop. As I got closer, among boxes of chocolate, cakes, and antique China on display, I noticed an adorable furry friend—a grey kitty with a red collar. What in the Hansel and Gretel's gingerbread house was this?

This was a feast for my eyes. If I could own a house adorned in my knits, serve dinner on flowery plates, and have cats roaming around, I could die happily. Oh, and let's not forget the cross-stitched frames with profane quotes to stupefy guests. Mei loved to say I resembled a grandma stuck in a twenty-one-year-old's body. Eh, I already missed her jokes.

When I entered, an elderly lady and her furry friend welcomed me. I took my Americano and three scrumptious mini cakes and sat at a tiny round table outside the café. It could've been the long flight or my inability to sleep on the plane, but the moment my lips tasted coffee, life became infinitely better, and all things seemed to settle in their right places. My momentary state of nirvana got interrupted by a whiff of the same earthy scent I smelled in my hotel room. I looked around, but most people sat inside the bakery, and no other person walked next to me. I began to wonder if there was a leakage of essential oils around here. "Petra, you're on vacation," I said to myself. "Stop trying to be an investigative journalist and focus on what you're trying to gain— memories. It's okay to focus on myself and maybe even suggested." I sipped the last remnants of my coffee, ate the last bite of my tiny dessert, and went to roam the old town.

A trip on the cable car took me to the highest point of the town, where I witnessed its marvelous view. A walk through the central square, which was embellished with a gorgeous fountain, and a walk to the Black church concluded my outing for the day. Mostly because my eyelids became so stubborn they refused to stay open. Sleep felt like the most alluring place to travel now.

The following day, the window was open again. This time I knew for sure it wasn't me.

CHAPTER 3

In my life, everything had to go according to plan. I hated discomfort and being taken aback by unforeseen situations, especially if I had to ask for help in said situations. So naturally, I picked the hotel closest to the Bran castle bus station. I could've gotten to the castle several ways: by train, taxi, or even renting a car. But the bus went through the town and nearby landscapes, so naturally, I didn't want to miss such an opportunity.

It took five minutes to walk to the Brașov-Bran bus station. Being early meant more space for me to enjoy my trip, but to my dismay, the station was packed. Since most riders were tourists, everyone wanted to sit next to the window, so I settled for the far back seat. For today's trip, I chose another comfortable outfit: the same jean shorts, same sneakers, same knitted crossbody bag, and a fresh T-shirt with the words "Stich Witch" sewn on it. And since my next destination was Bran "Let's Pretend a Vampire Lived Here" Castle, it seemed most befitting. Plus, I did have something in my bag resembling a book of spells.

My sister found it on one of our trips to Romania. I didn't remember much since I was only four and mainly was clinging to our mother's skirt. On the other hand, my sister, being twelve, loved exploring everything she encountered. One day, she wandered into grandma's dusty, old attic and found a box with a rusty lock underneath hay and spider webs. Without hesitation, my sister cracked open the box and found the booklet and a wooden apple. She loved to tell me this story over and over, and I listened to her as if she had discovered a new Atlantis in grandma's attic. When asked, grandma told us our great-grandmother used to sell homemade liquor, and one beggar who didn't have any money gave her the box in exchange for half a liter of *palinca*. Great-grandma, curious, agreed, only to be disappointed there wasn't any jewelry, just a small book, and a wooden apple, so she threw it in the attic, never to remember of it again.

But for my sister, it turned out to be the best find of her life, so she took the two dull objects to the states and never stopped bragging about it to all her friends or anyone gullible enough to listen, aka me. In time, the book's paper began to disintegrate, resembling an Egyptian papyrus with crumbling edges, while the apple had several cracks. Despite its frail state, we named it The Glinting Book when we realized it sparkled softly in the sun's rays. But not long after, my sister decided to keep the artifacts hidden and let me see them only when she was in a good mood.

As I got older, my sister told me she tried to decipher the incantations in the booklet. Each incantation's title was four random numbers like 1066, 1145, 1222, and 1301. My sister thought they were years, but we couldn't figure out what they meant. Having the library as the only resource back then, it took a long time to realize the book was written in a Latin dialect. When she understood some of the letterings, she taught me several incantations so we could pretend to be witches. If she were here with me, this vacation would've been a blast.

After several stops, a few locals got off the bus, vacating a golden seat next to a window. With zero hesitation, I jumped at the opportunity and snatched it. Finally, I could relish in the magnificence of the town's view. Brașov's gorgeous architecture had a lot of German influence, but when we got close to Bran Castle, the houses became more diverse. Some had two stories, and some had one. Most had red and occasionally green roofs, but the diverse façade made of either stucco, brick, or even wooden materials blew my mind. In the yard of one of the households, I saw a lady hanging laundry on strings. I could only imagine how laundry imbued in mountain freshness smelled.

If the housing infrastructure of Romanian cities kept the angle of my gaze straight, the fauna drew my eyes to a perpetually uptilted position where all the pine tree hills stood. Each tree looked like an exquisite specimen of its kind. The brooding mountain range resembled cyclopes in slumber, but I couldn't enjoy watching them for long as the landscape suddenly changed. Now we were welcomed by hills of sunflowers. I already knew from my father about Romania's astounding landscapes, but nothing could prepare me for the real thing. I began fiercely taking pictures. Who knew when I would ever return to visit again?

The closer we got to the castle, its grandeur felt more and more real. My eyes, thirsty for knowledge, didn't know where to look first. The pond, the wispy trees, the birds chirping, and the sunny summer's day, all contributed to the enchantment of the place, except for the tourists. Everywhere I looked, visitors from around the world scrambled to get through Bran Castle's gates. The path to the ticket booths had souvenir stands on each side, and people were drawn to them like bees to honey, more so than the actual castle. Sometimes, I wondered what reason tourists had to visit such places. To boast to everyone about it while presenting proof in form of a fridge magnet. Or to legitimately live and breathe for a fraction of time the way our ancestors lived hundreds of years ago. People needed to get their priorities straight.

I joined the line to the ticket booth, but half an hour in, I was only halfway through, and, this time, with an added bonus. The weather decided to throw a fit and began lashing down. Everyone scurried to buy umbrellas, only the price (based on market value) suddenly increased three times. It became a privilege to stay dry. Right when I accepted my fate to wait through the rain without an umbrella, someone tapped on my shoulder.

"A Romanian gentleman asked to gift this umbrella to you, miss," an elderly man with an English accent said.

"Where is he?" I asked, curious about the mysterious gentleman.

"Right there," he said, pointing in the opposite direction from the ticket booth. "Oh, I guess you missed him. I can't seem to find him anywhere."

I stretched my neck like an ostrich, trying to find Mr. Mysterious, but no one matched the description the older man gave. I looked at the umbrella, and its quality stunned me. It didn't resemble the cheap foldable umbrellas they sold here for the price of gold. No, it was a classic, straight umbrella I used to see in vintage movies. When I opened it, I could feel the luxurious smoothness of the wooden handle, and the frame had an undulated shape with a long, metal point in the middle. I had yet to see such excellent quality in an umbrella.

I peeked several times in the direction of my benefactor in hopes he would return. All the while, without realizing it, I found myself in front of the ticket booth's glass window. I paid for my ticket, handed the umbrella to a person from the back of the line, and climbed toward the main entrance alongside a group of tourists. With each step, my heart began beating faster to the point of wanting to run toward my childhood dream. The stories my dad told me and the memories he shared with his family visiting the history of his own country all came alive in my mind. I wished he, mom, and my sister could've traveled with me. Yes, this wasn't Dracula's castle per se, but it impacted my life far more than the cartoonish stereotypes many were familiarized with at an early age.

The castle looked carved out of stone due to its rocky foundation, while the top, in contrast, displayed intricate ornamentation. The towers were added later, at the beginning of the twentieth century, by Romanian royalty. Hence, some structures reminded most of a gothic style, creating the allure of a Victorian supernatural being's dwelling like Bram Stoker implied. As the tourist group, including myself, climbed the steep stairs slicked with rain, we entered through the massive arched doors into an entry hall. The walls, painted in a brisk white color, complemented the dark metal candelabra and wooden ceiling. The guide explained the tour's course, which included a secret passage and open balconies with a view of the mountain hills. At the end of our walk, we were to look closer at the stone well, the courtyard's centerpiece. The group and I followed the guide ahead through a hallway that opened to the magnificent castle's courtyard. With multiple entrances and exits, narrow paths, and windows small and large, Bran Castle resembled more of a labyrinth for the unaccustomed eye.

I observed how the tourists looked around as if searching for the spirit of Dracula hiding between the walls of Bran Castle. But considering the strong perfume one of the lady tourists spread, I believed any ghost lingering around had to exorcise itself to avoid the pungent smell.

Further inside, after walking another flight of stairs, we found ourselves in several rooms belonging to Romanian royalty. The rooms in colors of white, dark brown, and accents of red with nineteenth-century decor engulfed my vision. Once I let everyone else go ahead, including the perfume lady, I noticed the air's dryness. It was clean but dry. It always happened in places where no one lived, where people's tears and laughter didn't warm up the place anymore. Where a family's facets of life (even royal ones) were traded for thousands of curious footsteps and a home transformed from one's abode into a museum. But having the honor of witnessing history unfold, even in a sterile way, made my historian's heart leap with happiness.

As we entered the queen's bedroom, it mesmerized me to the extent of halting my walk and igniting my touristy spirit. I began taking photos of every corner of the room, hoping to never forget this experience. We walked through several rooms, including a Bram Stoker display, a dining room with a bookcase full of books, and a music room. Then we climbed on the castle's terrasse. I sat on one of the benches and looked through the photos I had taken earlier. The queen's room looked as elegant in the pictures as in real life. The bed, the candelabras, the throne, the furnace… "*Wait a minute,*" I thought, "*there's a spark coming from the furnace. Could there be a risk of fire?*" I had to find out.

My tourist group went ahead as I returned to the queen's bedroom. The rooms were empty for the most part, probably till the next cluster of tourists arrived. I didn't want to tell anyone yet, in case it was an absolutely normal thing for old furnaces to sparkle, and I preferred to avoid embarrassing myself. As I reached the temporarily silent room, I approached the stove and shined a light with my phone into the dark opening. To my surprise, it wasn't a fire hazard at all. It was a golden chain with a pendant. It resembled a four-leaf clover, somewhat larger than a quarter. The entire pendant was covered in crescent moon holes aiming in all directions. In the middle of it were four prongs meant to hold a missing gem. I wasn't sure if it was real gold or some gold-plated jewelry, but the little archaeologist in me could not let go of the piece. If I had found it, by old tradition, it belonged to me. Right? Right. I hid the piece of jewelry in my bag, spreading gusts of dust along the way. And like a rookie thief, I looked around for witnesses only AFTER hiding the prized treasure in my bag. Luckily, no one entered the room, and most of my group peers stood outside laughing and enjoying themselves. Never in my life did I commit a felony, but now knowing the thrill of it, I could sympathize with treasure hunters on a personal level. No pang of guilt could convince me to give away the discovery of my life now hidden in the depths of my bag.

I went ahead and visited the rooms left for me to see, but another type of scent appeared in my nostrils. If the previous one was balmy and earthy, this one had a sharp but dusty whiff. I looked around and, still, there was no one, till I realized the fragrance emanated from my bag. "Who knows? It could be that Romanians prefer to use essential oils everywhere. Who am I to question their traditions? At this point, I'm inclined to believe it's normal in Romania for windows to open on their own, for random strangers to gift umbrellas to tourists, and to find gold jewelry hidden in medieval castles," I whispered.

To avoid suspicion, I followed the same route as my fellow tourists and ended my visit at the antiquated well. I threw a dime in it, thanking it for the great blessing. Then, without waiting for the whole group to leave, I took a turn toward the exit, rushed down the stairs next to the pond, and plopped down on the bus stop bench. Not knowing how to act, I placed my bag in front and remained still while my emotions formed a whirlwind in my head. The guilt, the thrill, and the excitement pumped through my veins, spreading throughout my entire body. I took a few deep breaths in and out, desperate to calm my heartbeats. "*I didn't do it on purpose. It was blind luck. I couldn't say no to such an opportunity*," I thought, and then whispered, "today's adventure must end now. I better go to the hotel."

CHAPTER 4

The following day, I decided to rest after yesterday's unexpected turn of events. My morning afterthoughts did not match the previous adrenaline-charged excitement. Guilt began to bite at my conscience, and regret started to seep in. I took the pendant out of the bag and inspected it once more. Centuries-old dust still covered most of the chain and cross, but a few rubs with a cloth and the sparkle underneath reemerged. "It's clear I must return it. My dad taught me better than this. And the last thing I want to be called is a thief. I'll keep it with me during my stay. I'll inspect it, take pictures, and write down all particularities of the necklace. Then I'll return it," I said. Yesterday, I looked up something similar on the internet. The shape and craft of the pendant resembled an early 15th-century European style, specifically as part of a medieval queen's jewelry collection. This prompted the question: "How could a medieval pendant stay hidden in a furnace for so many centuries and never be found?" It boggled my mind, to say the least.

The furnace looked remodeled, so it must've been placed there in somewhat recent times. But by whom? And why? It could've been thieves who wanted to hide it in an unassuming place. "Was I a thief of thieves then? I hope not," I said, touching the pendant's prongs. Sadly, this one missed its gem in the middle. I wanted to place the pendant back into the bag, but the Glinting Book fell. The pieces looked as if they belonged together. If anyone incidentally checked my bag, they would think I had to be an artifact looter. If my sister sat next to me, she would be squealing with happiness and immediately figure out what to do next. My talents didn't include ingenious ways of getting out of weird situations. Ultimately, I put everything back in the bag and decided to visit grandma's old house in Poiana Brașov.

A short Uber drive from the city and into the mountains brought me to what, in the winter, would be a ski resort. Hotels, cabanas, ski slopes, and restaurants all aimed at a marvelous winter vacation, though summer didn't lack tourists either. After grandma's death, Dad and Mom knew we wouldn't return to Romania as our lives settled in the States. So, Dad decided to sell the house with its land to a restaurant owner. And since I always wanted to try authentic Romanian cuisine, I deemed it befitting to go to Stâna Sergiana, which was located on grandma's land. My entire childhood, Mom preferred cooking what she was best at, mac and cheese or burgers, and truth be told, they were part of my preferred regular meals, but, on vacation, I didn't want a safe-for-tourists menu. I wanted something new and unusual. I wasn't a picky eater, so few dishes could deter me from trying them.

After getting out of the Uber, from the corner of my eye, I noticed something scrambling toward my legs. When I turned around, it was a piglet. A piglet with a wet and pink snout and all. And not just one but a dozen. They roamed freely across the land with chickens and cats as their companions. "*Now, that is a welcome I didn't expect,*" I thought. The restaurant resembled more of an old-timey tavern. In the restaurant's foyer, the walls were made of rough wood logs while the décor took my breath away: shelves filled with dried garlic garlands, corn cobs, and large jars of marinated vegetables, on the floor rested massive, weaved baskets full of apples, an old wooden sleigh plopped in the corner, and goats. Real life, lazily chewing hay goats. I proceeded to tiptoe around them not to disturb their meals and hopefully avoid a physical confrontation with them.

The next door I entered led to a large two-story dining room. The décor continued the rustic theme with a centerpiece of three bears on a pedestal and a chandelier made of deer antlers. Still flabbergasted by my surroundings, I missed the server's question, asking how many would be attending. "Just me," I answered in Romanian. He smiled and accompanied me to my table, and presented the menu. Only then I noticed that each server wore Romanian ethnic garbs consisting of a white linen shirt and trousers with a fabric belt cross-stitched in a traditional pattern. "*I should try to stitch something like that on a shirt,*" I thought. I didn't want to waste time looking through the menu, so I said: "I would like today's special."

The waiter looked at me perplexed, be it from my "excellent" Romanian or food choice.

"Sure, it will be ready in about ten minutes. Would you like to drink something, miss?"

"Just water, please," I said. "*You're on vacation, Petra.*" I hissed at myself. "And a glass of wine."

"Very well," he said as he poured water into my glass.

Excitement filled my nostrils when I saw him carrying a bowl of soup and freshly baked bread. The smell made my stomach grumble as he placed it in front of me. When I began eating, I completely forgot about the server who still hovered over me. The delectable dish disappeared slowly with every spoon dip, leaving small rings around the bowl.

When I calmed my hunger, I took a minute to look around, and only then I noticed the server returning with the chef.

"Was the dish to your liking, miss?" the chef asked.

"Very much so."

"We're so happy you enjoyed it. Many foreign visitors usually refuse to even try it."

"What is this dish?" I asked curiously.

"It's called *ciorbă de burtă.*"

"It doesn't ring a bell. What is it made of?"

"Well, its main ingredient is cow stomach," the chef proudly said.

"What?" The baffling realization that I ate tripe soup descended upon me. "But I didn't taste anything unusual."

"It's our chef's masterful cooking skills," the server said, feeling more boastful than the chef.

"You must be a true Romanian at heart, miss," said the chef.

I didn't quite know how to react. In a way, the soup tasted divine. Then again, cow stomach? Blech. I thanked them both, paid for the food, and hurried to call an Uber. Tomorrow's stop: The Royal Court of Târgoviște, the real

Dracula Castle.

∞ ∞ ∞

The two-and-a-half-hour ride to Târgoviște differed in many ways from the one in Brașov. The bus, much larger than the previous one, carried various people on board. Grandmas with large bags and chicken pens, moms with toddlers trying to get closer to the exit, and teenage girls with eyes glued to their phones, oblivious of the surrounding chaos. After paying the driver, I dragged myself through the crowd and stood next to the girls. They hadn't noticed me, and I felt grateful to avoid the big ruckus in front. Even though the roads were perfectly asphalted, in the crammed bus, I felt every tiny bump like a crammed rollercoaster. And with every jolt, I was reminded of the artifact I kept hidden in the bag.

The previous night, nothing unusual happened. I had my dinner at McDonald's, just in case the tripe soup planned to send me on a reoccurring trip to the toilet. No windows were opened in the morning. Maybe the latch was broken, and they fixed it. Everything was normal except for the fragrance emanating from the pendant. I inspected it multiple times. It was impossible for the flat surface of the jewelry to hide a vial of essential oil. But its strong potency spread across the room, waking me up every time I tried to fall asleep. Only fear stopped me from opening the window. So, I accepted my fate for the night and kept my eyes glued to the ceiling the whole time. While wide awake, I realized the smell reminded me of the beginning of a storm when all the raised dust would mix with the humidity of the air. What could all this mean?

There was no time to find answers as the driver's loud announcement of the next bus station drew my attention back to my surroundings. Suddenly, a pandemonium ensued. Everyone had to get off the bus. The teens next to me pushed me to the side, and I fell on top of the chicken pen. The terrified chickens clucked fervently in response till a woman with a brown pixie haircut helped me get up and snatched the pen underneath me. When I finally sat in an open seat, I could observe the situation in relative safety, out of the locals and their livestock's way. The moms and their toddlers were long gone. The flutter of wings and the rattling pen were almost out, but the ignorant girls refused to let them pass through first. They simply jumped out, skipping half the steps. Last was an elderly man who thanked the driver for the ride and told him to say hello to his wife. And then silence. Oh, how I enjoyed the silence. Only three people were left, but I assumed they preferred quietude as much as me. Shifting to the adjacent seat closer to the window, I clutched the bag close to my body. A thief of thieves couldn't risk being robbed again. My newly formed thief pride wouldn't let me. I would've rambled about new carrier paths longer, but the view took my breath away.

Driving through Romania's countryside, one could encounter lands of corn, flocks of sheep roaming against an uneven, undulating woodsy backdrop, and chains of mountains enveloped in fog connecting them to the sky. A panorama of mountains, rivers, and serpentine roads, all part of a massive Romanian natural patrimony and all in one trip. My mind could feast on such imagery forever. But the steep serpentine turns had a rocking effect lulling me to sleep and unexpectedly reminding me how tired I was. As the bus kept leaning gracefully from one side to another, I drifted off into a deep slumber. I dreamt of a castle, a mountain, and a princess from medieval times. Her beloved prince gifted her the four-leaf clover pendant, but slowly he turned into a demon with red eyes and fangs longer than his chin. What in the Dracula nightmare was this? It woke me up abruptly, right in time for the driver's announcement of the final bus stop. I rushed to the exit, thanked the driver in Romanian, and got off.

The GPS showed the walk from the bus station to the palace took around ten minutes. Happy I had the time to enjoy discovering the city, I strolled the streets of Târgoviște in a relaxed fashion. Târgoviște was smaller than Brașov, with more single-story houses. In a way, the distinction between Transylvanian and Wallachian history can be seen even today. Nevertheless, each had a charm of its own. For the most part, silence dominated the town on a weekday afternoon, with an occasional car passing by. So, I let myself enjoy the songs of the birds and the ruffle of leaves. Then I heard someone walking behind me. I turned around to see who it could be, but the streets were empty. However, the moment I walked again, the footsteps commenced. Nefarious thoughts began cluttering my brain about foreign kidnappings and human organs sold on black markets until I felt someone's breath blowing at the nape of my neck. Scared beyond comprehension, I darted toward the palace ruins hoping to escape the threat I couldn't see.

CHAPTER 5

The arched entrance of the Royal Palace of Târgoviște stood gloriously in front of me, but unfortunately, I couldn't enjoy it to the fullest. I rushed to buy tickets at the booth. The lady, surprised by my frantic state, hurried to hand me one. After, I rushed to hide from the unidentified stalker behind the castle gates. I waited underneath the arch for several minutes to see if anyone would follow me inside. "*After, I'll probably get an Uber to drive me back to the bus station,*" I thought. "*But, for now, there's no point in fretting over something I couldn't even see. Let's enjoy this part of the journey. You've waited to visit this place forever.*" I dusted off my white maxi dress, drank some water from my favorite UW water bottle, and turned to witness the palace where my hero once ruled.

The brick arch I stood underneath had a marble plaque attached. On it were the names of all the Wallachian rulers who lived on the premise. I found Vlad the Impaler's name in the first line. He was one of the first and one of the bravest. I looked around and saw the patterns on the brick walls interlaced with cement reminding me of byzantine mosaics. Everything here was built with care. Once I entered, I realized the palace was only a part of a massive complex of buildings. Besides the main castle, which was in ruins, there was a church, a tower, and the servants' quarters. And even though, over time, several rulers built additional parts to the palace, the foundation of the original buildings remained.

I walked a few feet ahead, and an enormous church presented itself before my eyes. It glued my gaze to its multiple towers and narrow windows. Inside it were multiple paintings of prominent rulers of Wallachia. I couldn't read their names as they were written in an old-style font, but their images of grandeur did not escape my appreciation. Then there was another element that drew my attention, the smell. The same fragrance I noticed when the windows were open. To my luck, I saw a tourist guide passing by. "Excuse me. There is a notable fragrance in the church. Would you happen to know what it is?" I asked in Romanian.

"How interesting, you can still feel the smell even though this church hasn't had a service in hundreds of years," said the guide. "It's frankincense, young lady. It's usually burnt during church processions."

I thanked the guide, still a bit confused as to why frankincense persisted on the streets and through open windows, but I feared my questions would confuse him. Instead, I chose to focus on my visit.

After I got out of the church, I took a turn toward the palace's ruins. The path led me straight to whatever was left of the once magnificent castle: the vast cellar comprised of brick arches. One could grasp the opulence of the olden days only by their size of them. The brick walls were twice my height. I had to keep my head up to view the entire building. It imposed a contrast between the serene, blue sky above and the heavy history of the place. I walked down the massive stairs, partially covered by a transparent roof while several tourists came out of another room. I felt an inexplicable pull to go there. Its surrounding arches were more defined and spectacular. The closer I got to the walls of history, the more I noticed the dusty, stormy scent reminding me of the pendant. Could this place be connected to the jewel in some way? As my thoughts were preoccupied with its origins, my feet took me further and further away from other tourists to a more secluded corner of the cellar. It would've been entirely dark there if it weren't for the natural light illuminating from above. After admiring the structure, I was ready to turn back when I noticed something twinkling between the bricks on the wall a few feet away from me.

Curiosity took hold of me and brought me where a ray hit directly on what seemed like a precious stone. I tried to pry it open with my hands but to no avail. I took the army pocketknife my dad gifted me during a camping trip. I opened the knife and dug up the stone. It had a thick layer of dirt on it, making it hard to clean. A cloth I usually wiped my sunglasses with and some water did the trick. The stone turned from a brown color to a sparkling, oval-shaped, red gem with a golden streak running across its middle. It reminded me of a cat's eye stone, but much larger. For a moment, I thought it had fluid inside because it changed its colors in the light. "*Could this stone be part of some kind of ancient jewel? Wait a minute. What if I tried to insert it in the pendant I found earlier?*"

Given my previous experience, I glanced around for any prowling tourists. The coast was clear, so I took the pendant out of the bag. After failing to push it between the prongs, I took the handle of the pocketknife and pressed on the gem's corners, each at a time, till all four prongs fit perfectly in the once empty place.

"At last," I exclaimed. I looked at the masterpiece from a distance. The pendant indeed sparkled just like a medieval queen's jewelry. I took another look around. When I couldn't see anyone, not even the museum staff, I put on the pendant. Once it dangled around my neck, an inexplicable need came upon me. I felt the need to recite an incantation. The Glinting Book was still in my bag. I took it out with trembling hands, suddenly aware of a certain atmospheric pressure surrounding me. It opened it at the place where one of the papers was ripped, so naturally, I read the following one:

"Magnus omnipotens stella cadens,
Largire munus tuum super servum tuum
Fata resignantur, mea numina celant
Recludam librum temporis in quattuordecim centenis."

After saying the words, nothing happened, proving that the Glinting Book was nothing more than a gimmick. The fun lasted while we were kids, but I had to put on my big girl pants and accept the truth. All this was nothing more than pretend play, and it should stay so. Disappointed, I placed the booklet and pocketknife back in my bag, then tried to take off the necklace before anyone saw me.

Suddenly, everything turned dark. As if someone turned

off the sky's light. The walls around me began to shift. Massive gusts of wind began blowing in my face like I was free-falling, but nothing on my body moved except for my hair. As if invisible pages of a book made of strong currents blew through me, leaving me incapable of acting on whatever happened to me. The gusts' speed increased with every turning page, taking my breath away. Then it would slow down for a bit, and afterward, it would commence again, repeating the cycle repeatedly in a rhythmical tempo. It was impossible to determine how long it lasted as my brain blurred after several minutes. When I least expected it, everything halted. I fell to my knees. Still unable to grasp what had just happened, I fell asleep.

When I woke up, for the longest time, I couldn't remember what had happened. The darkness in the room was so impenetrable I couldn't even discern my limbs. I sat with my arms around my knees, trying to recollect myself from the stupor. Then I remembered my phone and noticed the strap of my bag still attached to my shoulder. I opened the bag, took my phone, and used its flashlight to shine through the premise. Though at first, my surroundings didn't clue me on where I could be.

I touched my face and noticed the pendant still attached to my neck. Fearing it could be risky to have something so expensive on me, I placed the pendant in the bag and used my phone's flashlight to find my way out of the place. But nothing could have prepared me to see an enclosed cellar. From the ceiling, water trickled along its walls, assuring the perpetual dampness and mildew of the cellar, which, in this case, intertwined with the dusty smell I experienced in droves. "Did I lose consciousness and was brought here, away from the heat? Could it be a hospital of some sort?"

I walked through the cellar using the beam of light as a guide until I stumbled upon a wall of wooden barrels. I went to investigate closer. I put my finger under the dripper and examined the liquid's dark red color realizing it was wine. An unusual feature for a museum to keep wine in its cellar. I brought the drop to my lips. The tangy taste and floral scent reminded me of one of the best glasses of wine I had recently at the restaurant. I walked a few more steps trying to figure out a way out, but nothing pointed to stairs or another source of light, just brick arches. They were the exact same as the ones in the ruin but newer. Every additional opening in the wall revealed another set of barrels. I didn't dare to check on those as I already felt like a trespasser in a different country. I wouldn't want to risk and find out what the repercussions were and what fine awaited me for even being here in the first place. After walking a few more feet, I heard voices not far, but no light I could follow. I attempted to run toward the sounds when I tripped on something heavy. My phone fell a few feet away, with its light upward still providing enough light to move around. I rushed to get my phone and directed my flashlight to the object I tripped on. I saw a large chain spreading across the entire place. Morbid curiosity took my legs further to see what was tied to the

chain. To my horror, I saw a skeleton in ripped clothes resting next to a wall. Some museums took it a step further, but this had to be a gruesome prank. What if a child was to run around here? The jolt of terror propelled me to escape the encounter, and to my dismay, I stumbled on the same chain again and fell. My bag and phone flew far in opposite directions. This time the flashlight turned down, plunging me into complete darkness. Another wave of sounds startled me. I turned toward its direction when I saw a tiny light shining from a flight of stairs.

"Finally, I can get out of here. I don't even know how I got here in the first place, but I definitely don't want to stay longer," I said.

I climbed the stairs with a spring in my step. As I got to the upper side, I looked around, but the place didn't resemble anything I'd visited. "Is there another fully renovated castle in town I didn't know about? Because this one looks as close to a real palace as one might imagine?"

As I walked through the narrow hallway, which maintained the same byzantine tradition as the cellar, I noticed multiple torches hanging on the walls. Windows were scarce, and the only ones I saw were narrow, rounded at the top, and made of mosaic glass. The researcher in me reveled in the accuracy of the building, but the woman in me questioned my safety. "How did I get here? Who was the person that brought me here?" These questions made my heart thump in trepidation. Something wasn't right. I felt it intuitively but couldn't put a finger on what. I didn't meet anyone for a good portion of my walk, and it felt like the castle was deserted. "Am I kidnapped? And why would it be in a 15th-century style castle?" I whispered.

The corridor walk felt endless until I saw two figures in the distance. They were men in armor. Was this some sort of medieval festival I got lost in? Everything seemed bizarre, but I couldn't pass on the opportunity to talk to the only people around. I needed to get out of here and back to the hotel by nighttime. The closer I got to the armored men, the better I could observe their attire. The accuracy up until the very last metal chain was astounding. The swords looked impeccable to the point of inducing unease, and for a slight second, I wanted to touch them out of pure curiosity. When I got closer to their backs, they still didn't notice me, so I patted one of them on the shoulder. The actor turned to me, unsheathing his sword, ready to slash me in half. His head lowered to behold me, and only then his shoulders relaxed. He then pointed out to his companion my clothes. He said something to his friend I couldn't catch, and they both started laughing, making me fold my arms in defense.

"Did you run out of a boyar's chamber, wench?" he asked in an unusual Romanian dialect.

CHAPTER 6

Perplexed by their behavior, I couldn't respond and simply stood there motionless, hoping not to trigger further suspicion.

"Or maybe she's a spy of Draculya trying to find out about His Majesty's affairs," said the other armored man.

"She could be both."

They looked at one another, pondering on what to do with me. While I wondered if my explanation would contribute to my benefit or completely ruin my chances of getting out of here. Without any regard for me, they grabbed my arms and began dragging me to what seemed like a dining room. The roughness of their hold, as well as the ignorance toward my presence, confirmed my suspicions. I was indeed kidnapped. The closer we got to the arched doors of the large room, I braced myself for a harsh judgment ahead till a woman's angry voice resounded behind our backs.

"What do you think you're doing?" the woman asked.

When the knights turned around, they released me immediately, giving me time to rub the soreness on my upper arms.

"She is a trespasser in the castle. We assume she's a

spy," said one of the knights.

"We want to present her to His Majesty so he can decide what we should do with her, old lady," said the other knight, less considerate of the elderly woman in front of them.

The stout woman wore a long-sleeved hemp dress in a dark green color, a vest with embroidered edges, and a dark brown apron reaching the floor. Her grey hair peeked underneath the white scarf tied to the back of her head.

"First of all, you are to address me as Mama Nica. I have been attending to the needs of this castle before you were born, young man. Second, how can she be a spy if she's dressed like this? Where would you find a sword? Under her chemise? Her day garments must be wet since today is wash day, and she was hurrying to finish her tasks when you two dolts stopped her from doing so," she said, pressing her fists on her hips.

"Do you know this woman?" one of them asked in an embarrassed tone.

"I know more about court matters than you'll ever understand. Now hand her over and go on with your duties."

When they released me, she gave me a nudge to keep moving in the opposite direction from the confused knights. "Can you imagine? Barely out of their mother's cradle, still wet behind their ears, and now they command as if they're lords," she said, walking faster than me.

With a quick step, we walked through what seemed like a never-ending hallway where everything looked the same. It resembled one of those ever-revolving snow globes, but the medieval version. The whole place smelled musty and damp until we entered the kitchen, and the aroma of baked bread took over any other scent. A rectangular dark wood table hosted a handful of women preparing food. One was plucking a headless chicken, another was cutting cheese, and another was placing the pieces on a clay plate. It looked like a preparation for a feast, all the while using basic tools. Next to them, an oven built out of squarish clay brinks generated a suffocating amount of heat to which no one paid attention. On top of a metal plate with a round opening stood a massive pot of boiling water. Every now and then, a maid would pour some water in a bucket.

The elderly woman seated me at the wooden table and asked the servant girls to give us space. She placed a reddish clay plate of bread and cheese, poured red wine into a clay cup, then took a chair and sat next to me. The moment I bit into the bread and cheese, I realized how hungry I was. As if the last time I ate were days, even weeks ago, but somehow my stomach never signaled it to me. My whole body awoke from a previous numb state, and only now, with eating, it began functioning again. I also realized my exceeding thirst, but scared of the repercussions of uttering a wrong word, I chose to point at the wooden bucket hidden underneath the table.

"Can you not speak?" the elderly woman asked.

I preferred to not answer, unable to decide which was best: to leave my identity unknown or expose myself completely. Maybe these people took part in an immersive cosplay experience, and me ruining their fantasy could not end well. Especially since they didn't even know me.

She got up, filled the cup with water, and placed it next to the wine one. I bowed my head in gratitude.

"Don't forget to drink the wine as well. You're pale as a ghost," she said.

I devoured the bread and cheese and gulped the water and wine in one go. It tasted the same as the wine in the cellar, but together with food, its flavor increased ten times. The elderly lady scrutinized every inch of me and, probably not reaching a satisfying conclusion, said: "My name is Anica Dinescu. Everyone calls me Mama Nica. I am the main cook here, but I also take care of the daily matters around the palace. The rulers might change, but we all need a warm meal and a clean bed to sleep in. I've been taking care of this place for many moons. Nothing escapes me, so can you explain how you got inside the castle? There is only one way in and one way out. You either got in with the help of a boyar or passed through the gates by hiding in a carriage."

Silence proved a great helper up until now, so I decided to keep it that way.

"Do you have a name?" Mama Nica asked.

I nodded.

"How will she tell you her name? She looks like she cannot speak," said a curly-haired girl.

"Who asked you, Smaranda? If she can't say her name, I will give her one," said Mama Nica.

I didn't react.

"So be it. If you do not know your name or cannot tell us, I will name you after Saint Maria. It's the name we give all nameless, orphan girls."

I shook my head and looked around, trying to find a way to explain my name. I grabbed a large rock close to the stove and showed it to the elderly woman.

"This is a *piatră*. Is your name related to *piatră*?"

I nodded slowly.

"Wait. As in Petra?"

I smiled at her and nodded faster, then got scared my reaction would make me suspicious and lowered my head.

She examined me inquisitively but then turned to the curly girl and said, "Smaranda, go fetch Petra some of your clothes since you seem alike in size."

"But Mama Nica, why me? I only have a few of my own."

"You want to recite the rules of being a good Samaritan again? Did the nuns not teach you enough?"

She looked between Mama Nica and me several times, then turned around in defiance and left the room. Mama Nica didn't even pay attention to Smaranda's burst of emotions and instead focused on my presence again. She took my hands in hers and examined them. "These hands haven't worked a day. Are you a noble lady?" Mama Nica asked.

I shook my head which made her even more conflicted about my presence.

"I do not have time for this." She released my hands. "If you are here, you are to work. All my girls were taken from the church's orphanage. No one knows where they came from. One could be the daughter of a boyar and another, the daughter of a peasant. In my eyes, they're all my daughters. And since we don't know who you are, and you cannot speak, I will treat you like one of my girls. Work starts at dawn before the roosters' first crow. We go to sleep after everyone in the castle has said their last prayer. We wash, pray, and go to bed. You will be given a bed and two meals a day. That's more than a peasant would ever dream of having. But here's where my Wallachian generosity ends–"

"*Wallachian?*" These people were serious about their cosplaying games.

"The moment I hear any trouble from you, be it a brawl or a nightly visit to a noble's chamber, you're out. I am not here to make justice or raise bastards. My girls know better than that, and so should you. We are not here to show who we are. We are here to serve those who put a piece of bread on our plates. I hope I made myself clear."

I nodded slowly, bracing myself and trying to make sense of all this.

In the meantime, Smaranda returned with the clothes. Mama Nica measured the clothes on my body and smiled approvingly. "Go to the girls' chamber and put on these garments. You are to help Smaranda today with carrying water from the well. In the winter,, we'll give you *opinci*, but since it's summer now, you'll go barefoo—" Mama Nica looked at my feet and saw me wearing my brown faux leather sandals. "When you are done, please fold all your other belongings and place them underneath your bed to keep the room tidy. Smaranda will show you the way," she said, implying something more with her eyes. In the meantime, I questioned what she meant by winter. I've never heard of yearlong cosplay events.

Smaranda turned toward the exit and to the back of the castle without regarding me whatsoever. I ran after her, fearing I might get lost and get in trouble with those knights again. I didn't have time to look around until we entered the servants' quarters. The girls' chamber resembled a large prison cell: one narrow window, no other exit except the main entrance, and simple wooden beds. The chamber's main décor was the cover, a pillow on the beds, and a small icon in one of the corners. The six beds were divided into two, with half on the left and half on the right.

Smaranda presented my future sleeping arrangement on the far right, then she turned around and left while I took a seat on my bed. It felt like nothing close to a mattress. The surface felt uneven and prickly. I peeked underneath the sheets, curious to see what stuffing they used. To my astonishment, it was dry hay. How was I supposed to sleep on this? Smaranda yelled to come out faster as more work awaited. I rushed to put the chemise on, which scratched my skin with its rough texture, tied the two threads sewn in the chemise around my neck, then added the double apron of even coarser material. One for the front and one for the back, and lastly, I wrapped a simple embroidered belt around my waist. After, I folded my white maxi dress, and in between the folds, I hid my brown sandals. If I were to survive the torturous cosplay event, I would have to live like a maid for now. All my belongings connected to my previous life had to stay hidden as far from prying eyes as possible. When I got out of the maids' chamber, Smaranda handed me two empty wooden buckets, turned around, and stomped toward the main entrance. I rushed to follow her steps to avoid losing pace and getting lost.

Outside, the change of scenery took me by surprise so much that I dropped the buckets. There had to be something wrong with my eyes. I simply couldn't believe what I saw. The ruins I saw mere hours ago came to life, turning into a real castle. The tower was there too, with a church added, plus a garden with flowers and many smaller buildings I wouldn't even be able to name. Either these cosplayers were millionaires investing a fortune in an immersive medieval experience, or I wasn't in my time period anymore.

CHAPTER 7

The realization clutched at my throat like a choker, limiting my ability to breathe properly. Smaranda noticed something had changed in my appearance but didn't deem it necessary to stop. I forced myself to lift the buckets and keep moving after her. The well didn't resemble the one I saw at Bran Castle. It was a spring pouring out of a carved stone wall. Several women washed clothes on a slab of rock near it. "*Ah, yes. It was indeed laundry day. Only in the fourteen hundreds*," I thought. We waited for several women ahead of us to fill up their buckets. When our turn came, desperate to cool down my thoughts, I hovered toward the water source and drenched my face completely. Smaranda pushed me to the side. "I always go first, sheep head," she said as she hurried to swallow a few gulps of water.

"It tastes best when it's cold," she said, wiping her mouth with the back of her hand. "You want to taste it too?"

I nodded, but she splashed my face with water when I leaned to take a sip. So much for hospitality.

"You think you can barge in our lives, Milady, and hope we'll share with you from the little we have?" Smaranda asked, placing the bucket under the water stream.

One by one, all the buckets were filled and ready to be carried. But I could barely manage to lift one bucket. Two seemed impossible to pick up. Smaranda took one in each hand and carried both at a fast pace. I didn't want to look weak by any means, so I took one and ran toward her, but when she saw me, she asked in anger, "where's the second bucket? What kind of a maid are you if you cannot even carry two buckets of water?"

I rushed the first bucket through the castle and into the kitchen, and then ran to get the second one. By the time I returned, I was ordered to bring two more.

Afterward, the day's work completely took away my awareness. I simply took orders and tried my best to fulfill them. If Mama Nica demanded to sweep or dust a room, the response was expected to be immediate. No further explanatory questions were allowed. And the requests never seized to stop: to bring apples from the pantry, to knead the dough, to run for water again, to wash the dishes in icy water, to pluck a chicken. All felt like bullets shooting out of Mama Nica's mouth. The only time I got excused from a chore was when I had to milk the goat. I didn't have time to realize I might not be very good at it till I pressed on the goat's teat, and it spurted straight into my eye. Anca, a tall girl, assigned to milking the cows and goats, moved me to the side and said, "I think you should help Mama Nica in the kitchen."

As I walked out of the shed, wiping milky tears off my face, I felt somewhat embarrassed but relieved. When nighttime descended, exhaustion crawled into my bones, and I could barely lift my arms and legs. But since that night, there was a feast in the Great Hall, several maids were ordered to cater to the nobles. Oh, how I prayed I wouldn't be picked. How could anyone do that after an entire day's work? Mama Nica chose a couple of girls I still didn't catch their names, while the rest sighed in relief. We went to our chamber to wash and then kneeled to pray before the small wooden icon attached to a corner of the room. One of the girls mumbled a prayer to St Andrew, the protector of the land, while everyone else held their hands together in front. When done with the prayer, she performed the crucifix symbol from forehead to chest and right shoulder to left. I repeated the movement awkwardly, hoping no one would figure out I didn't know how to do it. Then everyone changed their day clothes to a nightgown of similar fabric. I was given the scraggliest they could find, but my extreme tiredness made my body so numb I wouldn't feel the prick of a needle, much less some scratchy fabric.

I placed my head on the bumpy pillow, and right when I began to shut my eyes, one of the girls who attended to the guests at the feast flung open the door, sneezed first, and then said, "girls, you've got to see this."

"What is it, Teodora?" asked Anca. "Is the palace being attacked?"

"No, no such thing. There's something godly in the sky. A sign. It must be a sign." She jumped in excitement. "Who knows, I might get married this year."

By the time she finished talking, they were already out of bed, curious to see what Teodora spoke about.

"Well, why are you sitting there? Show us fast," said Anca, covering herself with a blanket. "But first, we need to tell Mama Nica, so we don't get in trouble."

I wasn't sure what to do: to follow them or was I supposed to remain in the chamber?

"What are you waiting for?" asked Anca, looking at me. "Cover yourself and come with us. We don't have all night."

With all exhaustion vanished, I rushed to get my blanket and sprinted through the door. Teodora was pointing to the sky when we and Mama Nica got out in the courtyard. "Look, the godly sign."

At first, I assumed it had to be a UFO. The multitude of sci-fi movies I watched has messed up my brain if I chose aliens as my first conclusion. In reality, it looked like a white ball with an enormous tail. Of course, it was a comet, and it looked stunning. Its tail, in the shape of a machete, spread across the sky, covering a third of it. I had never seen one before, and since I could see it with the naked eye, it must've been Halley's comet. But those got around Earth every seventy, eighty years. In my time, the comet had traveled before I was born, and it had many more years to pass for the world to see it again. This proved one thing, I was indeed in a different time period.

"It's God's sign that something will happen soon. Something big, and we must pray that His power will protect us. It could be a good sign for our ruler, Vladislav II. I just hope it isn't another earthquake," said Mama Nica. The lady possessed great intuition. If Vladislav II sat on the throne now that meant Vlad the Impaler wasn't yet the ruler of Wallachia. But sometime soon he would be taking the reign of the voivodeship and making life-altering changes for his people.

"When did the falling star appear in the sky?" Smaranda asked.

"It wasn't here yesterday," said Teodora and sneezed once more.

It was a great coincidence for me to have traveled to a different period of time, right at the moment when Halley's comet appeared first in the sky. "*Could all of this be connected somehow? I must go back to the cellar and retrieve my belongings. It's the only way I can find some answers.*"

We admired the sky for a long time until Mama Nica sent us all back into our chamber, as tomorrow's work plan did not lose in difficulty compared to today's challenging tasks. The girls wished good night to one another and went to bed. The moment my head lay on the hard pillow, I hoped sleep would take me fast, but after witnessing the comet, I finally realized I was far away from home. And it would take me a long time, if ever, to see my mom, dad, and Mei again. The thought made my heart clench in pain. Tears welled up and trickled down my roughened cheek.

I always wanted to experience the world of the people I studied in my history classes, but not to such an extent. The literal aspect of my research became far greater than I expected. The whole castle reeked of weird-smelling cheeses, mold, and dead chickens. Here and there, I could hear rats squeaking, and anything I touched had a rough surface that felt either itchy, spiky, or scratchy. The food tasted bland as if they put salt only in bread and on holidays. And it made sense since salt was expensive, and nobody knew better except me. This lifestyle was what they learned from the moment they were born till the moment they died. What I would give for a cup of hot coffee and a clean bed with a mattress. The only clean linen here covered the bed I slept on, and only because it stayed unoccupied for a long time. But the fooling white of my bed sheets camouflaged heaps of hay full of dust and dead bugs. Then again, who cared about basic hygiene when there was so much to do?

If I got stuck in medieval times, I had no choice but to adapt to whatever came my way and, who knows, maybe find a way to return home. No matter how much it pained me, I had to get over whatever unsettling feelings I had at the moment and focus on my return. First, I had to search the cellar and find my bag and phone. I had to learn my way around the castle to sneak in when everybody kept busy or slept. I knew the kitchen and a part of the courtyard. It may take a short time to get acquainted with the rest. As I kept planning my next move, sleep finally took over me.

∞ ∞ ∞

After two months of assiduous work with little to no time for a rest, I resigned myself to the idea of never getting back my belongings. Every day passed with the horrifying feeling that at any moment now, there would be someone who would find my bag. And rumors about a golden pendant in the shape of a four-leaf clover, an old booklet, and multiple weird contraptions would spread around. But each day, to my greatest relief, the rumor never reached my ears, giving me hope for the following one.

The issue wasn't the agonizingly harsh work conditions

or a schedule supported on only six hours of sleep. The issue wasn't sweeping, scrubbing, and dusting every corner of the castle, cleaning chamber pots, starting the fire in the furnace, cooking, or milking cows. It wasn't even the three-hour Sunday church service where we were supposed to stand the whole time, hold a candle, and pray (the hot wax falling on my fingers helped me stay awake on numerous occasions). No. It was Mama Nica's hawk-eyed, strict regimen of living. No maid could sit for longer than a few minutes. She liked to say sitting was for supper only. The chances of sneaking under her nose came close to null. I simply couldn't imagine going anywhere without her finding out. Smaranda tried a few times to do it and it ended with several slaps to the back from Mama Nica.

After a while, I would simply wake up, listen to the common prayer, eat, do my morning floor scrubbing routine, gather cabbage, onions, or garlic from the garden, carry water, help with cooking, perform a thousand menial chores, eat, clean my body with a cloth, listen to the evening prayer, sleep. It was sleep, scrub, snack, repeat. Nothing more. No thoughts, no attempts to change anything, just survive. Several times I've seen girls asking for help from their co-workers to ease their exhaustion, but I couldn't do it, and I didn't even know how. I mostly resumed my non-verbal communication to cats and other animals. Smaranda saw me a few times and snitched on me to Mama Nica, saying, "Mama Nica, she's feeding good food to the cats again. Mama Nica, she's playing with the chickens again. Mama Nica, she's petting the goat again. Blah, blah, blah…" What did poor Vincenta van Goat do to her to not deserve a cuddle? She was my only friend for the longest time, even when I did a poor job at milking her. She never complained and never tried to make me the scapegoat of her own wrongdoings like Smaranda. I don't know what the curly-haired complainer had against our friendship, but our bond would never be broken.

Though harsh, Mama Nica's strict schedule had several perks. No knight or stable lad would approach us because the threat of stumbling onto the old lady by accident terrified them. Her protectiveness gave us a sense of security in a world of injustice. Her harsh bearing had good intentions. She cared for us like for her own daughters, and our honor mattered most to her. Also, I gained enough experience to understand most of their archaic terminology. If English evolved considerably up until now, Romanian, for the most part, remained the same. The etymological roots kept the same Latin origin but with natural mutations across centuries. So even my rudimentary knowledge of Romanian helped me understand what they said and their underlying message.

The castle brimmed with royalty, from king Vladislav II and his wife to noblemen called boyars and their families, as well as knights who were part of the king's retinue. We loved to catch a glimpse at the ladies' ornate outfits: long, silky dresses in pearlescent colors, white headscarves, golden jewelry, and pearls around their necks and hands. I could see how the girls yearned to be in their places, if only for a day. In truth, the girls enjoyed living vicariously through castle gossip, but Mama Nica would always nip it in the bud and forbid us to even mention the nobles' names. Only when we happened to encounter a noble were we to stop in our tasks and bow our heads.

One time, Smaranda and I were scrubbing the floors in the hallway when we noticed the wife of a boyar coming our way. I rose to my feet to bow when Smaranda pushed the bucket, and the dirty water spilled in front of her. I bent on reflex to clean it up.

"You get up," the boyar's wife said. "You dare not bow to me?"

I immediately bowed, but it was too late.

"What do you have to say for yourself?" the boyar's wife said.

"She cannot speak, Lady Dobre," said Smaranda.

"You are mute and discourteous," Lady Dobre said and shoved a finger in my face. "Next time it happens, you'll end up on a bridge, begging for handouts from merchants passing through our lands."

I knew Smaranda held a grudge against me from day one. But I couldn't even use words to defend myself, and maybe my words wouldn't suffice in making her nicer toward me. Most of the time, she forced me to do her strenuous errands while she disappeared God knows where. But her torment reached a new level when she humiliated me in front of our superiors.

Unlike other maids, Smaranda wouldn't go to sleep right after the evening prayer. She would convince one or two girls to stay with her and gossip about the castle's internal affairs. Most of the time, they talked about knights and sons of noble families and how high were their chances of marrying any of them. That same night several more girls joined, including Anca, and she never stayed up late. She lit another candle, and with the added light, I had the opportunity to spy on them without getting noticed. So, I pricked up my ears and listened as I lay in bed, pretending to sleep.

"Have you heard?" asked Anca.

"What is it?" asked one of the girls.

"Our king went to battle with the past king, Vlad Draculya," said Anca.

"What?" A common interjection resounded.

"If our king loses, we might have Vlad, son of Dracul as king once more."

CHAPTER 8

The news of the impending battle between Vladislav II and Vlad the Impaler not only revived but also consolidated my hope of ever meeting my hero. I, unlike my co-workers, knew what the battle meant. The colossal events expected to happen in the castle and entire Wallachia would change many things historically. Many would not survive to tell the story. But even with cruelty lurking, if I could pick which time to live through, this period would always remain my choice.

"I heard Vlad Draculya's knights are the fittest and most handsome men in the land," said Smaranda.

"That's what they always say when a new king is trying to take over the voivodeship," Anca said.

"I cannot wait to look at them, even from afar," said Smaranda excitedly, "who knows, one of them might be my future husband."

"As if they will ever look at us," said Lia, the youngest, while braiding her hair in pigtails.

"I am so ugly, no one would dare to look at me," said Teodora, almost whispering. Her allergies had flared up, and she tried to hide her reddened nose.

"You never know how fate will turn around. I've been

praying to Saint Nicolae for quite some time," said Smaranda pulling a bottle of wine out of a burlap sack.

"Where did you get this?" asked Anca. "You know what will happen if we get caught."

"I'm but a foolish maid. What are they gonna do to me?" said Smaranda.

"You will be tried as a thief," said Anca.

"Mama Nica gave it to me," Smaranda said, taking a gulp straight from the bottle.

"I hope you are telling the truth," Lia said as she finished her pigtail braids and tied them with ropes.

"Listen, what do you think the new ruler will do? He'll release all the prisoners under the tower. He'll want to show how kind he is to his people. The best of times for us peasants is between changes of power. We might as well use it to enjoy ourselves a little," said Smaranda.

"How do you know Vlad Draculya will win?" Anca asked with skepticism.

"Even if he doesn't, our king will be so happy he defeated a pretender to the throne and the son of Dracul. The feasts will never end." Smaranda laughed. "Just because his father was part of The Order of the Dragon doesn't make him a Dragon. And didn't you hear how his father was killed? By Iancu de Hunedoara's own sword."

"What nonsense are you spewing? It wasn't Lord Iancu. It was our king, Vladislav II," said Anca, in her usual righteous way.

"Yea, well, it's not what the stable lad told me."

"When did you find time to stop by the stables and speak to the lad?" asked Teodora, taking the bottle from Smaranda.

"Hey, I went to the shed to get a few logs when I met him. He also told me about the new one." Smaranda pointed at me. "He saw her coming out of the cellar before Mama Nica brought her to us."

"But we're not allowed in the cellar. Only older men and Mama Nica can go. They even placed that skeleton there to scare the kids and us away for the same reason," said Lia, trembling at the thought of meeting Mr. Skeleton face to face.

If I could speak, I wanted to tell Lia, that as a sixteen-year-old, she was also a child but also, Mr. Skeleton was horrifying at any age.

"I know, but Mama Nica chose not to tell anybody about it," said Smaranda with an air of superiority.

"Is it so? Mama Nica said she was an orphan," said Anca, refusing the bottle and passing it along to the next girl.

"The wench doesn't talk. Mama Nica didn't have a choice but to assume she was an orphan," Smaranda said.

"Do you think she is mute, or is she pretending?" asked Teodora, trying to hold a sneeze.

Smaranda gathered everyone closer and whispered, "I think she's a *strigoaică*."

"What?" all of them exclaimed.

"*A strigoaică? As in the female version of a vampire?*" I thought.

"Few people suddenly climb out of cellars in unknown castles, especially a woman. She didn't even know what to do around the castle. I taught her everything. And when she smelled the frankincense in church, she acted like it was poison. She almost fainted a few times. Plus, she always refuses to eat garlic. And have you seen that dark mane of hers? She must be a *strigoaică* or a witch."

"I think she's kind of sweet," said Lia, but no one paid attention to her.

My dad used to joke about my mom being a witch since she put a spell on him, but I never thought I would be accused of being one in a literal sense. Didn't she know how scarce hair conditioners were in medieval times? I hadn't even taken an actual bath yet.

"You're just saying so because you're mad Mama Nica put her in your care," said Anca.

"As if that would bother me? I make her do my work while I go on the other side of the castle where the stable lad is." She cackled.

"You're awful, Smaranda. If Mama Nica finds out, you'll be boiling with the chickens," said Lia.

"Who's wasting candles in the middle of the night when people should be resting?" yelled Mama Nica from afar. "If you have time for chatting, I don't give you enough work." Mama Nica didn't even need to open the door to our chamber, the girls had already scrammed to their beds, and the light disappeared the second they heard her.

It gave me immeasurable pleasure to hear them huffing in their beds, scared out of their minds, but also, I couldn't let my sleep be interrupted, as there was work to be done tomorrow.

∞ ∞ ∞

Two weeks had passed since then. Smaranda feared angering Mama Nica after their drunken night and the consequential hangover the next day that limited their capabilities to work. Mama Nica probably knew everything since the bottle never got replaced, and she knew the exact number of wine bottles in the cellar. I presumed the incident turned into the first strike out of three, considering Smaranda's bootlicking behavior as we moved forward.

After the morning prayer, we were summoned to the kitchen for our daily instructions. Smaranda and I were assigned to scrub the hallways and clean the rooms on the East wing. We took a bucket of water and a couple of rags and went to the instructed area. When we arrived, she turned toward me and said, "how about you start on the hallway, and I'll go make the bed in His Majesty's chamber?"

I stood up and grabbed her by the forearm as she attempted to leave, shaking my head in disagreement.

"What are you going to do? Stop me? You fake mute. I know you can talk. You're itching to say something. Come on, say it." She shoved a finger in my face just like the boyar's wife.

I slapped her finger out of sight, and Smaranda took it as an invitation to attack me. She grabbed my hair and twisted my head toward hers. "What are you going to say now? Oh, I forgot, devil, got your tongue. Let's see, if I pull your hair a little more will you bleat like a sheep?"

I bit my lower lip in an attempt to muffle my screams. But not for long, as I grabbed her left arm and jabbed my nails in her skin. She only laughed at me, which made me angrier. I then hit her in the shin, and though not very successfully, she at least released my hair. I then pushed her down and began slapping the living daylights out of her. Smaranda kept laughing as if my hits resembled mosquito bites. She grabbed one of my wrists and turned them around very painfully. As my anger multiplied, I began scratching her face and biting her arms, which spooked her. She pushed herself out of my way.

"You are indeed a *strigoaică*," she said.

Before I could react to her words, Lia had already witnessed the altercation and ran to tell Mama Nica. I prepared myself for a stern admonishment but also wondered what Lia was doing in the castle's East wing. She usually helped Mama Nica with cooking and never left the kitchen in the morning.

Aware of the future trouble, Smaranda ran off to the kitchen to tell on me first as if I had a chance at telling her anything. Still, I raced her with the same intensity. By the time I got there, cursing my lack of stamina, Mama Nica had already heard what Smaranda had to say about me. She summoned me closer and then slapped both of us on the cheek. For a second, I thought her fingerprints would remain imprinted on my face forever.

"Are both of you out of your minds?" she said, aligning fists to her hips. "If any of the nobles would have seen you, you would both had your hands cut at best. Smaranda, what are you talking about Petra being a *strigoaică*? The only unnatural thing here is her waiting so long to put you in your place. Did you think I didn't know you're mingling with the stable lad?" Mama Nica grabbed Smaranda by the ear as she began to whimper like a puppy. "I hope you're not burdened with a bastard. Otherwise, you're out of the castle. Go work the land like other peasants and see if you find a morsel of food anytime soon. I've been good enough with all of you. Orphan girls either give themselves away for cheap or starve to death. God have mercy." Mama Nica rubbed her forehead in exasperation. "I sent Lia to summon you here since we have a new *voivode*. The messenger boy had just arrived to tell us the news. Vladislav II has been defeated in a one-on-one battle with Vlad Draculya. We must prepare for His Majesty's arrival. Now everyone must end their other tasks and do what I say. Teodora and Petra, you help Anca with the bread dough and anything she asks you to bring. Lia, see if the cheese is done. Smaranda, you go to the well and bring water. Once you're done, clean the stables, as you seem eager to be there."

The other girls laughed, infuriating Smaranda ever so much. She leaned in to fetch the buckets, glared at me, turned around, and walked toward the kitchen door. Not a moment passed when Smaranda dropped the buckets and stepped to the side as through the main door entered two knights in armor.

"We've come bearing good news. The true ruler of the Wallachian land has taken reign once again. Our *voivode* Vlad III Draculya, son of Dracul, will visit all chambers of the palace. Prepare for His Majesty's arrival."

CHAPTER 9

Mama Nica dragged Smaranda from the door entrance, pushed us all in a row closer to the stove, and said, "heads low and not a sound from any of you."

In my two and a half months of living in the Middle Ages, I underwent exorbitant physical labor, was humiliated numerous times, and had to accept the possibility of never seeing my family again. But, in that moment, my only concern was my inability to properly see Vlad the Impaler's face.

My gaze aimed at my dirty toes until I sensed the air changing. It became denser, more intense, and more threatening.

"Please bow to the ruler of Wallachia, His Majesty *voivode* Vlad III Draculya," announced a member of his retinue.

My breath stopped for a second, knowing I stood in the same room as my hero. When would such an occurrence ever happen? I heard steps coming from the entrance, and with every moment, they became louder. I peeked a bit and saw the tip of his boots. HIS boots. When Vlad the Impaler's imposing frame stood before me, I raised my gaze for a second. If I didn't, my sister would've never forgiven me. The blow to the nape I should've expected followed immediately.

"Forgive her, Your Majesty. She is new here and has yet to learn the rules," said Mama Nica.

He paused and said: "Let them look into the eyes of their true ruler."

I couldn't be more elated.

"Sire, we are but mere servants, undignified of such honor," said Mama Nica, bowing in front of him as she kept my head low.

So much for a meet and greet.

"So be it. Show me around, Mama Nica. How have things changed since my last rule? You must join us for the feast tonight…."

We stood motionless the whole while they talked in the kitchen. At last, when Mama Nica and Vlad the Impaler exited the room, we all exhaled a sigh of relief. On the other hand, I felt bitter that I didn't get enough time to take a closer look at my hero. Just a glimpse at his bushy mustache would've been enough.

The afternoon faded into the evening without respite. The request to prepare lamb took all of us by surprise. Work doubled instantly, but the meals for the feast had to be on the table by evening. Luckily, in times of urgency, we worked efficiently, and everyone knew their precise place in Mama Nica's kitchen. Smaranda kept the water coming, though she never went to clean the stables, and Mama Nica didn't have time to admonish her. Lia cut the cheese and placed them on plates. Anca baked bread. Teodora cleaned the dishes. While I was throwing more logs on the fire to roast the chicken and lamb. It was then that the realization came to me. For the first time since forever, Mama Nica would not be going to sleep at the same time as us, and I could finally sneak into the cellar and retrieve my things. The exhaustion disappeared, and the giddiness of holding my things once more reemerged.

At night, I already had stashed a small candle and the church headscarf in my wide, embroidered belt, avidly waiting in my bed for Mama Nica's footsteps to leave her room. The night turned into a "retrieve the bag" mission, and I couldn't wait. When I heard each of the girls' deepening breaths, I took it as a signal to leave the chamber. I chose to remain dressed in my white flax nightgown for more leverage. Black attire might've been a better choice, but I doubted anyone would notice me. The graveyard shift knights guarding the castle usually directed their attention on outside threats, not on a measly castle servant. Plus, everyone genuinely celebrated Vlad Dracula's return.

The first time Vlad the Impaler ruled only for a month before Iancu de Hunedoara, the regent of the Hungarian Empire, and his father's killer threatened his life, making it impossible for him to stay. When Hunedoara died of the plague this year, Vlad viewed it as an opportunity to return to his throne. I knew, for a fact, his second ruling would be his longest and most prolific. They had a great reason to celebrate. Most of the details I remembered were from when I studied medieval history, but I needed a fuller picture. If I wanted a better chance at survival, I had to study in greater depth what happened during Vlad's second reign. I had to retrieve my phone and the portable charger from my bag. "I hope they didn't deteriorate during the time travel," I whispered.

The hallways, though only lit with torches, didn't represent a challenge anymore, as I could walk through them with closed eyes. I could not say the same about the cellar. I remembered only parts of my walk from back then, but I needed to know exactly where my bag and phone fell. The fear that someone might've found them already still pulsed hard in my head. The easy part of the scheme was that the cellar stood right at the castle's entrance. The difficult part was I had to get the keys to the cellar, which hung on a nail in Mama Nica's kitchen on the other side of the castle. Overall, I had to run four times across the castle. To take the keys, to open the cellar and retrieve my belongings, to rush back and hang the keys back in their proper place, and then to return to the servants' quarters.

On my first run, I heard voices from the depths of the night's silence. I wanted to run back outside, but the voices weren't moving, making me believe they came from the Great Hall. I saw a light protruding through the door as I got closer. I already knew I had to walk next to the Great Hall, but it didn't occur to me they would keep the door open. "*Great. More challenges.*" I tiptoed close to the opposite wall to keep my presence in the darkness. Once the coast was cleared, I sprinted to the kitchen and grabbed the key. On my way back, I could hear only one voice as I approached the arched doors. I knew the dangers of prying into other people's business, but I couldn't stop myself. Because based on the strong oratorical inflection in his voice, I already knew who spoke:

"I wish this land to be that of the Wallachians. Not of

their neighbors. Not of their enemies. A world belonging not to traitors, not to thieves, but to those who want to fight for their land till their last breath. But first, we are to give all a chance at redemption. The prisoners at Chindia are to be released, and all their deeds forgiven—"

I peeked through the cracked door, and there he was—Vlad the Impaler. Of medium stature, the ruler of Wallachia greatly resembled the portraits available to us in the present day. He wore a pointy red velvet hat embellished with rows of pearls around its base. On top of the pearls, an eight-pointed golden star was attached to it, with a ruby in the center. Above the star, a feather featuring five larger pearls gleamed in the candlelight. The most prominent feature on his face had to be his nose. Of an aquiline shape, the nose alongside his mustache gave Vlad a menacing demeanor. The long curly hair might've softened his facial aspects if not for his greyish eyes and arched brows, which implied a cunning aspect of his personality. He rose from his throne wearing a red tunic with large gold buttons looking like he carried the whole nation's dignity. I admired him and feared him with the same intensity.

He never broke eye contact with his men, all seated on each side of his throne. Only a few stood next to him, and I could see their faces clearly: two older and two younger men. I wanted to move ahead with my plan, but Vlad's intense charisma nailed me to the floor. When would I ever have the chance to be near THE Vlad the Impaler, son of Vlad Dracul? My sister would jump in excitement if she knew.

All of a sudden, I felt someone's stare. Relief flooded

over me when I saw Vlad carrying on with the discourse, never raising his gaze, but then I caught another from one of the younger men seated next to the throne. He looked straight at me. I hid behind the door, hoping it wasn't me he noticed. But when I slowly returned to the same spot, the man kept looking straight at me while the corners of his mouth rose. He flaunted one of the most stunning and irritating smiles I've ever seen. I couldn't risk staying at the scene any longer. If he told Vlad, I was done for. I might be the first one he'd impale.

I stepped back and around, avoiding the light beaming from the door's opening. A flickering shadow would announce the whole gathering of my presence. Then I turned toward the cellar, lit the candle from one of the torches, and rushed down the stairs to the familiar moldy smell. Guided by candlelight, I took a better look at my first encounter with this world. I felt a sense of nostalgia for the person who didn't know what awaited her. In a way, I still wished to be innocent again and confuse my travel across time with just a cosplay event or an overdone prank. I walked to the chain I tripped on before. It didn't seem as big or menacing as the first time.

I then followed it to where the skeleton dwelled, but there was nothing except sacs of grains and barrels of wine. Maybe Vlad ordered to clean it up. I wasn't sure, and it didn't matter. I simply wanted to find my phone and bag. Fear gripped me again. What if someone did find it? No, the whole castle would've known. Of that, I was certain. After a three-sixty-degree rotation around the premise, I got a clear view of my surroundings and noticed something twinkling into the pit of darkness. It had to be my phone. I jumped in excitement and rushed to grab it. Though I knew there wouldn't be any sign of life coming from my phone, I still pressed the home button. I missed the feeling so much. "Now, where could my bag be?" I whispered.

Unfortunately, besides the few reference points like the chain and wine barrels, there was no clear indication of where my bag could be. I only remembered it flew in the opposite direction of the phone, and there I went. The further I wandered into the cellar, the more I realized its obscurity turned it into a labyrinth. I halted a bit when the candle began melting and burned my finger. I didn't have long. Ideally, it would have been to go through all the corners, but there wasn't enough time, and I had to get some sleep before the new day's work started. The only plausible path guided me further and deeper into what felt like a cave. The mildewy stench got stronger, making it harder to breathe, and the droplets of condensation multiplied. The rat squeaks, which would've made an anxious mess out of me two months ago, didn't bother me more than the buzz of a mosquito. I tiptoed a few more steps, and right when I questioned the ability of my fragile candle to guide me back, I tripped. This time, on my bag. The jubilance at that moment made me squeak so loud it reverberated through the narrow walls producing a prolonged echo. I hugged my bag as if it was an old friend I never thought I'd see again. I looked through my belongings: the pocketknife, my ticket, my wallet, and finally, my portable charger. My water bottle must've remained in the future. As I dug deeper, the glimmer of the pendant shone before my eyes. I put it around my neck and ran toward the place I once time-traveled. When I found it,

I closed my eyes and repeated the incantation, just in case. But nothing changed. Furious, I took it off and shoved the pendant back into the bag. At least I had my other belongings. It was more than nothing. But now I had to get back to my chamber. It was too dangerous to stay there for long. I placed my phone in the bag, zipped it, pulled my headscarf out of my belt, and wrapped it around it.

The walk back felt lighter and easier. I knew exactly how to get out, thanks to the unintentional candle trail I left. After climbing the stairs, I hastened on the previous path through the castle. I expected to hear voices coming from the Great Hall, but to my delight, silence reigned the castle's hallways. When I got closer, the Great Hall, cloaked in the dark, gave me the much-needed green light to get to the kitchen. In one slick move, I hung the keys on their respective nail and returned for my final walk to the servants' quarters. The imminent success of my mission narrowed my gaze to a tunnel vision. My focus aimed only at running as fast as I could to my chamber and into my bed. I didn't even care about the candle. I had left it in the kitchen. With a bright smile enough to eclipse the torches and eyes looking past my immediate surroundings, I hit a wall.

The collision happened so forcefully that it flung me on my back. When I looked up, it didn't take long to realize the wall I stumbled upon was a man's chest.

"Are you alright?" the man asked.

"Yes, thank you," I said as he pulled me upright.

"You have an unusual way of speaking. Are you the daughter of a Saxon?" he asked, surprised.

Oh no! I spoke at the most inopportune of times. In

desperation, I pretended to not notice him and continued my walk like a friendly little ghost. But when I attempted to walk away, he quickly grabbed my arms. "You're not leaving anywhere," he said.

At that moment, I knew I was done for.

CHAPTER 10

He pushed me to the adjacent wall underneath a torch, tucked a hair strand behind my ear, and took a closer look at me. My heart began pounding, piercing through my composure. The embarrassment of being caught sent heat waves through my body and stopped on my burning cheeks. The entire time I lived here, I never felt so exposed as the moment he glared into my eyes. Still, I couldn't help but notice another unwanted feeling emerging underneath layers of fear and panic. I noticed his dark eyes, the golden streaks glimmering thorough his black hair, and the mischievous smile which mirrored a devilish cunningness greater than Dracula. Then again, nothing in a million years could convince me to recognize how attractive he was.

"I saw you lurking behind the door of the Great Hall, listening to an important speech. I thought I should return. Maybe the dainty intruder shall return once more. My intuition didn't deceive me. Are you one of Mama Nica's girls?" he asked, pausing for a second until the realization came to him. "You must be the mute girl everyone is talking about. Well, they didn't mention what a charming voice you have. Probably because I was the only one honored enough to hear it." He snickered.

Without saying a word, I turned my face away from him. Upon noting my defiance, he loosened his grip. I saw it as an opportunity to escape, yet when I tried to break free from his constraints, he pushed me back to the wall and pressed his arms on both of my sides, invading every last inch of my personal space. My bag, wrapped in the scarf, acted as the sole barrier between us. His hold on me wasn't as physical as much as visual. He immobilized any of my movements solely with his gaze. It felt like he bore into my mind, thoughts, and ambiguous feelings. I had to break loose from whatever intentions he persuaded, so I lowered my head to his chest adorned in leather and metal rings. Without his visual domination, I became victim to all my other senses: the feel of his thumbs barely grazing my arms, the sound of his deep breaths, and the traces of cedar wood emanating from him invading my nostrils. The unwanted feeling from before began pulsating stronger in my brain. "Why am I attracted to this guy who called me a 'dainty intruder'?" I curled up around my bag to put more distance between us.

"Why are you cowering? Are you hiding something behind the scarf? Is it stolen goods?" he asked as he tried to pry my bag from me.

The insolence, the audacity, the arrogance. How dare he? He could plaster his delectable eyes in my face as much as he wanted, but it would never convince me to let him rummage through my belongings and make me lose my only chance at getting home. Mama Nica thoroughly informed me about the castle knights' womanizing reputation, and I didn't have time for drama or relationships, especially dramatic relationships.

One thing I've learned from watching too many videos on body language was how to disarm any adversary in the simplest way: with a wide smile. He might've been a tall, dark, and (somewhat) handsome medieval knight, but I had modern technology on my side. I grinned my most genuine fake smile and he fell right into the trap. He stopped in his tracks but continued to search for an answer on my face. I raised one of my bare feet and felt my way slowly up his leg. He approved of my action. Of course, he did, the arrogant bastard. His shin seemed an appropriate target for an attack, plus I garnered sufficient experience with Smaranda. I kicked the spot with the fury of a thousand maidens fooled by the charms of handsome knights and disarmed him completely. He groaned in pain and began jumping on one leg like a maimed rooster. I didn't wait to see my actions' repercussions as he seemed to recover fast from his injury. I sprinted so fast out of the castle I felt like flying. I already imagined myself hiding underneath the covers of my bed, where I could finally relax and calm the strong heartbeats and frazzled breaths.

With one disaster averted, another one loomed in the servant's quarters. One prying pair of eyes would be enough to get me in trouble. As I opened the creaking door, my heart dropped like a boulder. A light flickered inside the rooms, but to my surprise and hope, it didn't shine from our chambers but from Mama Nica's room. "She must've returned from the feast and is getting ready for sleep." I tiptoed to the maid's chambers. The girls' soft snores welcomed me. I hid the bag underneath my pillow and jumped into bed, but when I turned toward the door, the light in Mama Nica's chamber still glimmered. With a bit of apprehension, I decided to look and see if everything was alright. No response followed after my first knock. I knocked again, and finally, I heard heavy steps dragging along the floor.

"What are you doing here, in the middle of the night, Petra? You long to work so much you came to ask for more?" she asked with a chuckle.

I might've been an idiot prior and blew my cover, but not the second time around. I kept my mouth zipped and gazed at her inquisitively. She looked at my facial expression of worry and let me in. In the few months I've been here, I visited Mama Nica's room maybe twice, and it felt like discovering a new world every time. Besides the bed in the left corner, the room overflowed with wool yarn, rugs, and rug-weaving contraptions. Some rugs were displayed on the walls, but most were neatly folded beneath a wooden table. A water basin with an off-white cloth inside stood in the middle of the room.

Mama Nica noticed my curious glances and said, "a few rugs are for my niece's dowry. She lives in the village, but the rest are for you, girls. For when you get married. A bride without a dowry is a bad sign. So I'm weaving a rug here and there when you girls give me some time. Come sit with me." She took my hand, nudged me to sit on her bed, and then went to the basin to wash something. "A boyar at the feast spilled a goblet of wine on my Sunday belt. I'm trying to save it," she said, rubbing the stained cloth fervently. But every time she did so, several embroidered threads ripped.

I went to the messy table next to the bed and opened a

wooden box. Mama Nica had one of these in almost every room around the castle. From inside it, I pulled out some thread and a crooked needle. Mama Nica furrowed her brows in confusion. I picked the embroidered belt from her, brought it closer to the candlelight, and began stitching the bald spots.

"Careful, it is my most expensive belt," she yelped. I placed my hand on hers to calm her unease. She let me. We stood in perfect silence, with her peering at my handiwork while I focused on doing something I enjoyed.

"You're not a simple maid, are you. You're not even from our lands," she said, confirming something she already knew.

I glanced at her in surprise but went back to sewing, pretending Mama Nica's intuition didn't comprehend the situation so well.

"I do not know your aims of hiding in foreign lands but know one thing. If the higher-ups know you're not but a mere servant, your life will be in danger. Under my wing, no one will dare touch you. And if you wish to marry on this land, be sure to find a good man. One who cares about you first and then about the world's treasures," she said and began coughing uncontrollably. The old lady ran to the table, scooped a spoonful of honey from a clay jar, and swallowed it.

"At night, the coughs get worse."

I never knew Mama Nica was sick. She appeared stronger than a bull. And I'd never heard her cough so intense during the night. Then again, exhaustion acted stronger than sleeping pills.

"When my good husband died years ago, I wished God

would take me with him. He was the light of my life, but he left me so early and with no children. I wished to leave this world as his bride. For days, I wept at his grave, in the blistering sun, and during storms. My body almost became numb to the pain when my sister and niece ripped me from where I wished to die. I lay in bed with a fever for days, praying for my body to release my soul. But death never came. And I had to find the reason why God let me live. The reason became my girls. I went to several monasteries and…," she looked at me as if woken up from a dream. "Why am I telling you this drivel. Death will be the final path for all, except for the strigoi."

As she finished talking, I handed her my reconstructed masterpiece.

"It is late. Tomorrow is another long day. Go rest," she said, placing her hand on my shoulder as a sign of appreciation.

Behind the closed doors, I could still hear Mama Nica's coughs.

∞ ∞ ∞

Dawn hit me like a pile of bricks. I could barely keep my eyes open at church, and I only cared for the cup of warm milk and piece of bread allotted at breakfast. Why was coffee introduced so late in Europe? I would've killed for a freshly brewed cup of coffee. I would've smothered that guy's smirk on his face for a cup of instant coffee. A worthy transaction, I might add.

When I entered in my usual somnambule state into the kitchen after the morning prayer, I noticed the sun's rays spread their light spears across a man's head. For a moment, I thought it had to be a saint descending in the figure of a handsome man. "Wait a minute, a man?" I rubbed my eyes to ensure I wasn't having a nightmare. It was indeed a guy, a young man in Mama Nica's kitchen. And not just any man. The guy from last night. I was doomed. Next stop—the stake. I halted my steps, and all the other half-sleeping post-praying companions stumbled into me like an unfortunate game of domino.

"Girls," Mama Nica said in a syrupy voice. "This is Gabriel. The son of Mircea Stoica, our Sire's second in command."

All the girls gathered in a semicircle to revere the young knight who purposively used the morning light to his advantage. The girls didn't stand a chance. They were one step from becoming fangirls. All of them began arranging their disheveled locks and smiling like idiots as if he would notice anyone with a lower status than his.

"Sit, girls, your cup of warm milk is ready. The loaf of bread is on the table, rip a piece and eat. Fill up those bellies. You have a lot of work today," said Mama Nica. She seated me on the edge of the bench where underneath a piece of bread hid a chunk of cheese. I looked at her in disbelief. She smiled and whispered in my ear, "eat. You need the strength." The old lady then took the arrogant bastard by hand and seated him right next to me, forcing me to shuffle further from my initial seat. The smell of leather and cedar attacked my nostrils once more.

"Here you go, my boy," she said.

"You like to spoil me, Mama Nica," he said with a radiating but very annoying smile.

"Well, what can I do if you come to see me on rare occasions?" She patted him on the shoulder and plodded back to the stove.

He turned his gaze toward me while I began gobbling up the food like a wild boar. The quicker I could get out of the kitchen, the faster this would end. Smaranda went to Mama Nica and asked for another cup of milk which she gladly offered.

"Yesterday, she told us to keep those bellies empty till we finished work, and today, we can ask for seconds," Smaranda whispered, making everyone giggle. Mama Nica, indeed was in a better mood.

I, on the other hand, kept my face low and moved only when necessary.

"I remember when Gabriel was but a young boy of seven. Running around the castle after the ladies' girls and fighting with wooden swords," she said as she continued to pour milk into his clay cup. "Now you're probably running around fighting Turks and catching thieves, huh?"

Upon hearing those words, the mouthful of milk I so eagerly gulped went the wrong pipe, and I began coughing profusely, spilling milk all over. Of course, everyone took a good look at the idiot who couldn't even drink fluids properly. They all began pointing at me, and even Mama Nica stopped.

Gabriel, though, took a rag and wiped the mess I made, his actions calming the ruckus. He came closer to me to wipe a breadcrumb from my face and whispered: "A guilty conscious needs no accuser."

I swallowed a big lump of air, took the coward's way out again, and ran. Then I remembered I needed the bucket of water and rags for my morning cleaning routine. So I had to return in complete humiliation since Mama Nica's wrath was worse than meeting him again. I entered the kitchen, trying my best to keep a stealthy pace, but even if my ninja skills would've been at an expert level, the skirt's hem undoubtedly ruffled up some noise betraying my presence. Still, I behaved aloof and went to get the wooden bucket next to the stove and the rags.

Gabriel thanked Mama Nica for her hospitality by kissing her hand. What a knightly and gentlemanly gesture. Or better said, what a fake gesture. Faker than me and I was a time traveler pretending to be a servant in a medieval Wallachian castle for crying out loud. I poured some water from another freshly brought bucket, then went on my merry way as if nothing had happened. I thought I had escaped the whole situation, but then I felt my bucket get lighter, and, for a moment, I thought it broke and spilled water all over the place. Again. But when I looked at the bucket's handle, another hand was holding it.

"Would you like a helping hand, Petra? Or should I say, little imposter?" He beamed.

I ripped the bucket from him, almost spilling it on me, and rushed to the castle's East wing.

"Are you willing to drench yourself and not recognize that you can speak?" He ran after me.

Even if I wanted to speak, I would never talk to such an arrogant jerk. Eager to avoid him, I entered the chambers of Boyar Dobre. Upon entering, I stumbled upon the boyar's wife, Lady Dobre, taking a bath. The aroma of essential oils imbued the air and my nostrils and made me dizzy.

When the lady saw me, she said: "What are you doing

here, servant? I do not wish to be bothered. Leave."

I retraced my steps, unsure of my footing until I hit a wall aka Gabriel's chest. "*Why does this keep happening to me?*" As I turned around, my only hope was for him to not notice my disheartened state, but when I saw his illuminating smile once more, I froze. It looked like he carried the daylight on his broad shoulders. It made my heart skip a bit again. "*I must be sick. It could be some serious heart disease.*" I couldn't let him pursue whatever plan he had in mind, so I tried to distance myself. I had walked a reasonable distance when he grabbed my elbow and pulled me back to his chest. His mouth came close to my ear and whispered:

"If you want to keep your secret safe, meet me at the castle's gate after everyone else is asleep. I advise you to listen to your gut and obey my words."

I shuddered at his words and feared to even look at him. By the time I turned around, he was gone.

CHAPTER 11

The whole day went in a mindless drag, from scrubbing the floors to mixing ingredients for the bread dough. All the while, his threat festered in my thoughts. If I were to listen, God knows what he could do to me in the middle of the night. He could rape, kill, and chop me into pieces. I've watched too many true crime documentaries on the subject. And given the times, few would even notice I went missing, maybe Mama Nica and Anca. I could already hear Smaranda's gloating cackle at the news of my disappearance. Then again, he was a knight. There had to be some dignity hiding underneath his armor. A codex or something. Plus, if I didn't go, my days had a death clock attached to them, ticking the last hours of my life. Hiding in the church proved pointless, and praying to St Andrew would not save me. As much as this palace seemed big, me trying to hide in it resembled a hamster hiding in his cage. Everyone could see me.

I ruminated long on the subject while kneading my fret into the bread dough. Afterward, at the evening table, Mama Nica noted with delight how soft the bread tasted and praised me. She also said she looked forward to tomorrow's batch. "*Too late for that*," I thought. "*My tomorrow might never come.*" During evening prayer, I prayed for an easy death. Considering the medieval populous' love for torture, a rapid death might be considered merciful. I combed my hair, put on my nightgown, and went to bed first, pretending to be tired. Which wasn't a lie, but the sparks of anguish wouldn't let me rest even for a second. I hoped the girls didn't plan their usual gossip chat, but as per usual, things didn't go my way. The girls blabbered their way into the night, oblivious of the fretful torment towering above me. But then I remembered the knight didn't specify when I was to be there. My presence was required only after everyone fell asleep. I had a good reason, but would it be enough to escape punishment? After an uncomfortable amount of time, the candle went out, followed by bed sheet ruffles and, ultimately, heavy breathing. That was my cue. I got out of bed, pushed my hay-stuffed pillow under the cover, braided my hair, put on my day clothes (to give at least an impression of decency), and sneaked out the door.

As I rushed to the main gate, fear turned into surprise when I couldn't find anyone, not even a guard. For a moment, I thought he had tricked me. Then I heard a voice. I couldn't distinguish whose it belonged to, and fear took hold of me again. I began retreating when a hand gripped me, one I inadvertently learned to recognize.

"You're here," he said in an excited tone.

"*Why would I not be here after you threatened me this morning?*" I growled in my thoughts.

"Come. Stan, here, will help us."

"*Help with what?*"

A man emerged from the shadows of a tree, but only

after Gabriel called upon him. Stan, a muscular man in his thirties, approached us while holding a spear and a round shield, wearing a chain mail with a leather vest. His serious demeanor changed when he saw Gabriel, but without much talk, he went back to his assigned post and began rotating a lever releasing two coiled chains attached to the wooden gate. Even though it squeaked immensely, none of them seemed to be bothered by it. What if the noise would wake up His Majesty and the boyars? Or worse, Mama Nica?

As the wooden gate unwound, crashing to the ground, Gabriel took my hand and ran across the newly formed bridge. I had never been outside the royal courtyard, but what I witnessed resembled the backdrop of a fairytale about dragons, medieval castles, and knights. I already knew I wasn't in my time period, but I still harbored a speck of hope deep in my heart that maybe outside the walls of the Palace at Târgoviște, everything would stay the same as I remembered. And maybe, it would be the end of some madman's game. Alas, I was wrong, but the disappointment didn't last, as I once more accepted my reality and let my surroundings sway my attention from the menacing knight pulling at my hand. After crossing the first bridge, another one followed. Two moats and two rows of stakes sharp like pencils encircled the palace.

The double protection made me realize the significant measures Vlad the Impaler took to maintain some form of independence. A glance further away presented several rows of small houses and a massive amount of trees, making it feel like the town was situated in the middle of the forest. As if the Romanian woods were our landlords and we were but meager renters. The starry night with the full moon as its central piece bestowed upon us a view beyond imagination. The lack of city lights which usually diluted the prominence of the night's light made the contrast between the black sky and stars far greater and alluring. It felt like a reward for my relentless work at the palace. The end of summer had a way of emphasizing the best of nature's beauties. I followed the guided path with eyes glued upwards. Only when Gabriel's pace slowed down I lowered my gaze to witness the end of the bridge and a horse tied to a wooden stick hammered deep into the ground. He must've planned it all out, probably not only for me. He rushed once more, be it from excitement or worry, pulling me with him. After untying the rope, Gabriel checked the saddle's reliability and mounted the horse. The way he swiftly moved from an upright position on the ground to a seated position on a horse impressed me, but I questioned where I would fit, as there wasn't another saddle for me. Before I could figure out an answer to my question, he swept me off my feet and pulled me straight into his lap. I began wrangling myself out of his hands, refusing to agree with placing me in such close proximity to him. But then he whispered in my ear, "I understand you might not agree with such seating prospects, but I do not have a second saddle, and I can assure you riding behind me without one would convince you in a breath to relinquish the squirm and enjoy the ride in front."

I shot him my meanest look possible but didn't say anything.

"And next time you wish to express your disdain, use words. I presume you have plenty." He smiled mischievously.

Oh, I had an overflow of words ready to be spewed in his face, but the moment I opened my mouth, he gripped the reins and whipped the horse who responded by galloping at full speed. After an embarrassing scream, I tightened my hold and nestled deeper into his chest. Modesty lost its importance in the face of imminent danger.

I nudged him to slow down. He didn't listen and said, "you'll have to ask with words."

I felt my anger rise uncontrollably like the bread dough I made that morning. Especially when I saw his smug face smiling and relishing in his trickery. But only for a short time. He might've thought of me as a weakling, but little did he know about the self-defense videos I watched religiously. I learned a thing or two about how to cause pain with minimal effort. The wind blew through my hair, making it hard to distinguish what he had underneath his shirt, so I began patting him alongside his arm. I assumed the gesture pleasantly surprised him as he didn't attempt to stop me. I placed three fingers above his bent arm, and on the fourth, I dug my finger as hard as possible where I hoped it was a pressure point. He jolted in pain, losing one of the reins in the process and almost dropping me.

"A feisty one, I see," he said with a laugh. "So be it. I will slow down." He calmed his horse to a trot, and I could finally raise my head from my newly formed burrow. I tamed and adjusted my hair away from my face to determine where we were. It seemed we reached a higher point as I could observe far greater territory than before. The view differed so much from my first encounter with Romanian towns. Numerous houses and asphalted roads which occupied the hilly landscape not so long ago disappeared. The few houses and maybe one or two long pebbled roads illuminated by the moon were barely visible underneath the immense greenery. In this time period, it looked like humans still lived in the cradle of nature's blessing. He sped up slightly. The same wind, which at high speed lashed my face, now caressed my cheeks softly. I could've enjoyed the caresses much longer, but the horse came to a halt awakening me from a state of tranquility.

When he dismounted the horse, I could finally witness our journey's destination. It was a river. A wide, fast stream with trees hovering above it on each side. We were in the depths of a woodland, dark and uninviting, except for the small meadow leading up to the river. What was his intention, though? Did he bring me here in an attempt to sleep with me? And if I were to agree (which I would never do in a million years), where would it happen? There wasn't even a bed here, just pine needles, rocks, and ant hills. Or maybe he wanted to see me naked? Or maybe he simply wanted me to enjoy a swim? Heck, I hadn't had a relaxing day in months. Maybe he brought me here from the goodness of his heart?

I almost believed in his good intentions, but such a statement would be far from the truth. Because if he indeed possessed such a thoughtful character, I wouldn't be left stranded on his horse in the middle of the woods. I didn't expect him to carry me, but a helping hand would be the least he could offer. The scoundrel! He tied the horse to the closest tree, then dashed across the meadow without paying me much attention. He would disappear behind the shadows and then reappear in the spots illuminated by moonlight. Close to the shore, he began undressing item after item: his red embroidered belt, white shirt with red embroidered cuffs, boots, and finally, his linen trousers. I could catch only a glimpse of his body, but from what I could discern, he looked magnificent. In a game of shadow and light, the prominent muscles of his body danced with every move. The picturesque view of him as a central figure resembled the painting of a Roman God. He lowered himself slowly (maybe too slowly) into the water, swam a few times, and returned to the shore, looking at me and making me feel self-conscious for ogling at him.

I had to face my fear. Good thing the horse was calm and didn't really care about my presence on his back. I grabbed onto the saddle and jumped off rather unladylike. But who cared about being a lady in the middle of the night in the depths of a forest hundreds of years in the past. I tiptoed to the river, fighting off my additional fears of snakes or other crawlies my bare feet might encounter.

"Come join me," he yelled, waving a hand toward me.

How did he imagine me doing so? Get naked as well? The swimsuit had a long history of evolution ahead.

"If you're shy, I can turn around," he said and did exactly so.

Not in a million years would I skinny dip with some stranger in the middle of the night, no matter how much he resembled Adonis. Still, my body hadn't experienced a fully-fledged bath in months, and the twinkling light reflecting the stream's waves called upon me like a siren. It would've been perfect if I could extricate him from the picture, but ignoring him had to suffice. I had to choose between my integrity and the acute desire to submerge myself in a body of water. The latter won. I stared at the not-so-chivalrous knight in case he lied about not peeking. He wasn't. I took off my embroidered belt (nothing as intricate as his) and my front and back aprons, leaving me with only a chemise. I untied the knot at my neck and took the hem from my ankles and over the top of my head. The late August night breeze traversed my naked body, enveloping me in a warm embrace. When it stopped, hot air inundated my skin, compelling me to imagine how refreshing water had to feel around my body.

"Are you ready," he asked, turning his head.

"No," I yelled, desperately trying to cover myself.

"Well, now she speaks."

CHAPTER 12

How I despised this man. I shot him a menacing look and said, "if you do not turn away, I will not go into the water." The scoundrel smiled but obeyed my request. Feeling somewhat assured, I tiptoed close to the riverbank, this time fearful of stepping on something sharp. As I got closer to the stream, I tested the water with my big toe. It was ice cold. How in the world did he swim so comfortably? I didn't want to look weak to the point where cold water could deter me from taking a swim, so I went toe by toe, inch by inch, into the icy bath. My whole skin resembled a plucked goose skin, but at least I preserved my pride.

When the water reached my shoulders, my body adapted to the temperature quickly. I could finally relish in the immersive state of swimming. Reveling in my newfound comfort, I sensed a shadow approaching. It was Gabriel's mischievous smile reflecting the moon's light. "*Oh, why, oh, why did he have to be so handsome?*"

"How is the water?" he asked.

"Good," I answered, still in awe of the experience (I wasn't sure which one).

"I like hearing your voice," he said and began

swimming closer to me.

All my danger signals began beeping in my head. To avoid confrontation, I started swimming backward as he approached me. He probably did this with many women, including noble ladies, all the while expecting something in return. Well, not from this newly formed servant. I'd rather eat pine needles.

"Do not fret. I did not bring you here for my personal gain. You can trust me. You have a knight's word of honor," he said, raising his hands to show his sincerity.

While I assessed his honesty, his body began submerging fast into the water.

"Swim. Swim," I yelled, exasperated.

He didn't listen, so the next moment, he sank fully underwater.

"I believe you. I believe you. Please move your hands," I squealed. Without thinking, I went in to try and save him, but out of nowhere, a hand grabbed me by my waist and yanked me under. Seconds later, we resurfaced in an embrace. He held me so tight I could feel his heartbeat.

"Thank you for saving me. I don't know what I would have done without you," he said, exposing his teeth in an expressive smile.

I pushed myself out of his grip and put some distance between us.

"You didn't need saving. You did it because you wanted to…to trick me," I said, trying to find words in Romanian.

"The caring hands of a woman can save any drowning man," he said.

"Or push him deeper into the water."

"I think you're improving. I can understand the words

you speak," he said, swimming closer to me.

Fury encompassed me. How dare he? Being limited in my weaponry of retaliation, I chose the only thing that was at hand and in abundance. I splashed him. Not just one splash, but a whole tsunami flooded his face. He, of course, didn't let me win without a fight. The splash battle of the strongest had commenced in the waters of a Romanian river. He wanted to stop me by grabbing me from behind, and after my previous experience, I wasn't going to let it happen. So I swam in the direction of the river flow, allowing the current to move me faster. He didn't falter for a second and joined me in the race. The further we swam from our base camp, the darker it became. The banks rose higher, and the trees had their roots exposed which looked like monstrous creatures. In my heightened state of awareness, I began hearing different sounds, from the hoot of an owl to the rustling of leaves along the river's trajectory. A shiver of dread went through my spine as I flowed deeper into unknown territory, but I didn't want the bastard to know it, and in no case would I ask for his help, so I let the current take me further in hopes of finding a riverbank close by.

"Where do you think you're going?" He caught me by my waist. "As much as I like to play cat and dog with you. It is unsafe on this side of the forest."

"Why?" I asked.

"If you don't know, it means you've never lived on these lands before. Sometimes, it's best to stay in the unknown."

His entire demeanor changed from the previous boyish playfulness to a man who knew more than he let it be seen.

I turned back, but swimming against the current after the earlier efforts, became a real struggle. After a few minutes, exhaustion took over my body, but my pride didn't let me own up to it and confess. It took a single glance for Gabriel to realize it and offer support by latching on to my waist and resorting to swimming only with his right hand, whereas I treaded with my left. In a team effort, we finally reached our camp.

Panting in exhaustion, we got to the shore of the riverbank, but to our surprise, we had visitors. I raised my head up to notice a deer sniffing me. I yelped, alarming the deer and Gabriel in the process. When we looked further into the meadow, we realized we were surrounded not only by a herd of deer but also by other forest animals like rabbits, foxes, and wolves. Up on the trees, every branch held sparrows, crows, and owls. They all stared eerily at me as if waiting for a command. I froze, not knowing what to do. Gabriel realized they all followed only my movements, so he sneaked past them and put on his clothes. He then grabbed my garments, mounted his horse, and trotted as close to the shore as possible. I, on the other hand, did not know what to make of these hypnotized animals. They were not aggressive or hungry. They simply stared, following my every move.

I felt a deer's wet snout sniffing my toe, which made me flinch and run for dear life. I didn't even have time to put on my clothes, so I jumped like a distraught Eve from the clutches of an eerie Eden and into the hands of Adam, who WAS fully clothed. He then signaled the horse, and we galloped at high speed away from the peculiar danger. The animals and birds didn't follow us, but they watched us until they vanished from my sight.

When the dangerous situation felt far enough, my cold body made me realize my embarrassing situation. Gabriel realized the same thing. He slowed down the horse, handed the reins to me, took off his shirt, and pulled it over my head. I slipped each arm into the oversized sleeves, regaining a bit more dignity but a little less pride in the process. I felt the warmth inside his shirt, as well as the warmth of his soul.

Gabriel stopped the horse after it felt safe. I jumped off, still drunk with adrenaline, put on my chemise, wrapped around the aprons, and tied my embroidered belt around my waist. All the while, he kept his head turned the opposite way. He returned his gaze with a smile when I told him I was done. I gave him his shirt back but noticed he didn't have his boots on. "You forgot your boots."

"I'll collect them tomorrow. The woods are like my second home."

"After what happened today?"

"Such things don't usually happen during daytime."

"Does something like this happen often? How is it possible for so many animals to gather in one place?"

He remained silent for some time, unsure if he wanted to delve deeper into the topic. "There's more to the woods than a simple man could explain. Sometimes it gets out of the bounds of what feels like the real world."

I didn't find any meaning in his words but based on his tone and seriousness, I decided not to pursue the question further.

We rode the last part of our journey at a more relaxed pace. At the gate, Gabriel knocked three times, and the sound of squeaking chains began unraveling again. Stan greeted us and said, "are you back already?" He glanced at Gabriel and tried to imply something more.

"The weather cooled off," Gabriel answered in an unperturbed manner.

"You don't say?" Stan said mockingly.

Gabriel chose to not react and simply handed the horse's reins to Stan. "I'll be back for my turn." He placed his hand around my waist and walked me to the servants' quarters. Halfway through, in one of the darkest corners of the green patch of land, he stopped in his tracks behind an oak tree. I was unsure of what the evening and its events meant, so I looked at him inquisitively. He then grasped my face in his palms and pierced me with his gaze. The kiss happened on its own. I didn't have time to think or react, and by the time I realized what had happened, it was too late, so I simply let myself be swayed by the touch of his lips. They tasted sweeter than I imagined, as if dipped in honey and myrrh. It transcended every expectation I had, and I could compare not in years but in centuries. And for the first time, in what felt like forever, I wanted to let myself enjoy something or someone while relinquishing the fear of tomorrow's day. I wished with fervor to be caressed by a hand that cared for who I was and not because of something they expected in return. Gabriel exuded that feeling, that deep sense of security. Something in my gut told me I could rely on him, even at the worst of times.

But there was also a new sensation blooming inside. A feeling I had never felt before. As if his mouth on mine were meant to be together. A long-lost part of me that had finally reconnected. The impression of belonging, of an ingrained invisible tie. The solution of a jigsaw puzzle the size of a lifetime. All of a sudden, fear engulfed me once more. This new feeling scared me. I didn't want it to permeate my thoughts, my body, or my chance of ever returning home. So I pushed him away. He didn't seem surprised. Instead, he looked grateful and excited for something that maybe felt out of his reach.

"I have to go," I said, and without waiting for his response, I turned around and ran toward my chamber.

When I reached my room, I noticed a light escaping underneath one of the doors. It didn't come from Mama Nica's door like last time but from ours. "*Why would the girls be up at this hour?*" Smaranda jumped in front of me when I opened the door, holding my pendant: "There is the thief!"

CHAPTER 13

"She's a thief, I tell you. She's pretending to be mute and now I have proof she's a thief." Smaranda pointed at me in disgust while addressing the other girls.

I wanted to remind her of the time she accused me of not only being a thief but also being a *strigoaică*, but sadly I couldn't confront her about it either. I scanned the room to see if Smaranda found the rest of my treasure. I knew I could offer a plausible explanation for the pendant, but in no case would I be able to weasel myself out of explaining the existence of a phone. To my relief, in her mind, my greatest misdemeanor stopped at the pendant, and I got a chance to live another day.

Smaranda dangled the jewel in front of me as if I wasn't humiliated enough. Enraged by her audacity, I lunged at her to take the pendant, but she was swifter on her feet and dodged my attack. My fall, which resembled a clumsy clown's trick garnered a few laughs and more humiliation on my part. Great. Just great.

"Now you're showing your true face," Smaranda said, cackling. "I knew she was a spy and thief. Look at her trying to hide her true nature."

Already fed up with the Smaranda's theatrics, Anca stepped between us. She snatched the pendant from her and said, "everyone to bed. Now!"

Everyone jolted at the sudden authoritative tone of Anca's words and jumped into their rectangular hay havens. Except Smaranda who tried to take back the prized possession, but Anca being one of the tallest girls in the castle wouldn't have any of it.

"Why are you on the enemy's side? She stole from our nobles. Where do you think she was up until now? Sneaking in noble men's rooms, stealing, and God knows what else," said Smaranda.

"And why were you looking into her things?" asked Anca. "Mama Nica will be the judge of you both tomorrow. Now it's too late to fight. Go to sleep."

While Smaranda tried to convince Anca to take a side, I raised myself from the floor. With a bruised elbow and ego, I glanced at Anca in gratitude and made my way to the bed.

In the end, Smaranda capitulated and went to bed still fuming. Once the candle was blown out, silence befell. My mind, on the other hand, raced through all the medieval history books I read trying to recollect all the torture methods usually preferred by Eastern Europeans. I prepared myself mentally for the worst. A single stab to the heart, a nipped carotid artery, a broken neck came close to mercy at this point. Unfortunately, medieval people loved a spectacle and given the limited amount of entertainment they received daily, an execution came closest to being one.

On these kinds of days when everything seemed to go awry, I missed my sister most of all. She always found a way out of any preposterous situation. If only she was here.

Even with the gruesome scenarios my future days entailed, my utter exhaustion still managed to put me to sleep.

When I woke up, the girls were gone. The sun shone high in the sky denoting I overslept. "*Why didn't anyone wake me up? Not even for morning prayer?*" I changed into my daytime chemise, tied my apron and belt, wrapped a scarf around my head, and rushed to the kitchen. All the girls already worked on preparing lunch for the nobles, except for Smaranda and Anca. With a somber demeanor, they sat at the table across from Mama Nica. Smaranda spoke, while Anca and Mama Nica listened to her arguments about me being a spy, a thief, or both. I began walking toward them when Smaranda jumped and pointed at me. "There she is."

Mama Nica looked at me inquisitively, trying to figure out from my facial expression if the snitching toad was right.

"Smaranda is telling me you have stollen a piece of jewelry from the nobles. Is it true?" Mama Nica asked with a disappointed tone.

I grabbed her hand and shook my head vehemently, hoping to convince her of my innocence.

"This is something I cannot decide on my own. I must speak to His Majesty or a noble," she said, arranging her woolen vest. Mama Nica hid the pendant in her embroidered belt, and without much consideration pushed us to the side and went to fulfill her mission.

"Now you're in trouble. You shouldn't have angered me and maybe all of this wouldn't have happened," said Smaranda.

"Off to work," said Anca, "there is no time to spare. You've been slacking all morning. Smaranda will work with Teodora today. Petra will help me with carrying water from the well."

Boasting with pride, Smaranda sauntered to the stove. I, on the other hand, held my head low and followed Anca to the well. This adventure of mine had to end sooner or later. Might as well happen now. I wasn't equipped to survive the harsh medieval environment and let's be real, I never stood a chance of getting home alive. But even with the threat on my life, I couldn't help but think of Gabriel. How disappointed he would be when the rumors would inevitably reach his ears. I already feared looking into his eyes.

"I don't think you are a thief or a spy," said Anca, waking me for my brooding state. "Smaranda is the one to lie and then pretend to be holier than thou. We're all like sisters here, but she was never sisterlike. The girls were still children when Mama Nica went to a nunnery close to the castle and asked for girls who didn't fear working hard. I joined a year later when my mother died, and I had to help my father and siblings. Her plan was to teach us the ways of the church and castle early on. One time, I asked Mama Nica why she didn't choose of few boys as well. She said boys had a better chance of making it into this world. Girls never did. Though I still had a family in the village, Mama Nica became the mother I needed. She raised each of us to appreciate the gifts we were given even in the toughest of times.

"Well, everyone but Smaranda. When I first moved to the castle, Smaranda fought to prove me or anyone who listened that she wasn't an orphan, and it was treachery to force her to scrub the castle's floors. Smaranda wasn't supposed to move to the castle, but one of the nuns asked Mama Nica to take her as a favor. Still, Smaranda didn't show any gratitude, but kept saying her noble Saxon parents would find her, and she will order to punish us all."

I giggled at the thought and Anca mirrored my reaction.

"I'm glad the story made you feel better. Who knows? Smaranda could've stole it and then hid it under your bed. But do not worry, not everyone is like her. If something, I can help. You are like our sister now. Or, at least, a good friend," she said and went ahead with two buckets full of water.

Her words stunned me. I never expected Anca to care about me so much. It made me want to tell her the pendant truly belonged to me and Smaranda didn't have anything to do with it. But where would the explanation lead me? Definitely not to a time traveling person from the future. They would consider me a witch and would grant me the prize for witchcraft in the Middle Ages: death.

Without Mama Nica's sharp commands, we spent the entire afternoon in silence and worked in a rather sluggish way. To balance the laziness of my movements, my inner-self trembled like a leaf in a hurricane. How would my life turn next? Would it destroy any chance of ever returning home?

By the time Mama Nica returned, we were almost done with dinner. Weird how she stayed so long in the company of nobles as they usually imposed a superior air in front of anyone except their own. Then again, Mama Nica wasn't just anyone. Who knows? Maybe they all feared her, just like us.

For a moment, I only saw her entering the kitchen, but as she got closer to us, a wide shadow appeared behind her.

"I looked for His Majesty and any of his commanders," she said.

At the sound of her words, my heart began pulsing faster.

"But most are on an expedition to visit the king of Hungary. I was fortunate to find anyone," she continued.

Heavy steps followed Mama Nica and in came a massive man dressed in a yellow tunic and a leather vest with fur at the edges. His salt and pepper colored hair and short beard were well kept as well as his manicured hands which held my pendant high and in everyone's face. His name was Boyar Dobre. It was how he preferred to be called. Other than that, I knew few things about the noble, except him being Lady Dobre's husband and a womanizer. My presence never made an impression on him, as I mostly avoided contact with him and his embittered wife. This time, unfortunately, he knew exactly who I was, so he didn't hesitate to call upon me to come closer.

"Mama Nica is telling me that this jewel belongs to you," he said, shoving the pendant in my face. Like husband, like wife.

I didn't answer.

"Why isn't she answering?" He turned toward Mama Nica inquisitively.

"The Lord took her voice," she answered.

"Oh, even better. Nothing makes a woman more graceful than when she can keep her mouth shut. A mute woman is a close second." He rubbed his hands in excitement, but quickly regained composure.

A shiver of disgust went through me, destroying any hope of him not being the sleazy old man his reputation preached.

"I must keep a close eye on the maid and conclude if she is a threat to the castle." He turned toward Mama Nica. "I will have to take this young lady to my chambers. I must speak to her in private."

"As you deem, my lord," said Mama Nica in conformity, but the whole atmosphere resembled that of a mother sheep giving away her little lamb to the big, bad wolf. "But she must sleep in the servant's quarters as per His Majesty's orders."

"Do not concern yourself with such a trifle issue. The girl will make her way to her cot soon enough," he said gloatingly.

Dejected, I followed the boyar's wide shadow to his chamber. Nightfall protruded through the narrow frame of the window, making it hard to see his room, but from the few lit candles, I could discern a large bed, a fireplace, and a desk. The chair next to the desk looked like a wooden throne resembling a smaller version of the one in the Great Hall which belonged to Vlad the Impaler. As he sat at the finely carved desk, he placed a few yellow papers in front of him and began scribbling something with a quill. It seemed like he wished to make an impression on me. Once he finished scratching the parchment and placed the quill in the inkwell, he turned his attention toward me. He leaned on the back of the chair, interlaced his fingers, and examined every inch of my face and body as if trying to decide how he should act from now on. I tried my best to not look at him and kept my eyes on the floor.

"It is a little hard to decide what we're going to do with you." He rose to his feet reducing the distance between us. "From one side, you could be a measly thief that stole an expensive jewel of Hungarian royal origin—"

"*Of Hungarian royal origin*?"

"—or you are indeed a Hungarian noble woman hiding from her usurpers behind the walls of a Wallachian castle. And since you are willing to scrub floors all day, the crime must be considerable."

I lowered my head, realizing that none of these theories bode well with me staying safe and alive.

"Do not worry, little dove," he said, raising my chin with his manicured fingers. "The honor of my nobility will not let such a young and defenseless creature like you fend for herself. If you choose to become my consort, I will secure a place for you in this castle."

I stood corrected. A tortured death wasn't the worst thing that could happen.

CHAPTER 14

I took a step back to distance myself from his hands and this situation.

"If I say that you are thief, under the new law, you will receive capital punishment. Gone were the days when one could get a fair trial or waste their days behind prison bars. Our new ruler made sure of that. So, there's not much of a choice. What do you say? You want to keep your pretty body the way it is or dangle on a stake and become crow fodder."

I didn't react which he took as a sign of approval.

"Wonderful," he said and smiled lasciviously.

If I could find Gabriel, maybe he would know how to get out of this sticky situation. But after yesterday, he might've taken my running away as a form of rejection. I hadn't seen him all day, so maybe he intentionally chose to avoid me.

"But first we must clarify the matter with His Majesty. He will have to judge if you are a thief or an honorable woman. Though I'm sure, Vlad will listen to my words of support. Then we will present you as my consort," Boyar Dobre came closer and hid a strand of hair behind my ears.

The gesture resembled that of Gabriel's the first time we met, except for the dread I experienced throughout my entire body.

I knew it was legal to have multiple consorts in medieval Wallachia, but never in a million years would I have imagined me becoming one of them. Now I understood why Lady Dobre soured so much. Given her husband's affliction for younger women, I probably wasn't his first or second potential consort.

"Sadly, he and a few of his men went on an expedition to the kingdom of Hungary and who knows when they might be back, in a few days or weeks," continued Boyar Dobre.

Now that he mentioned it, Gabriel must've joined the expedition. Then nothing could be done. I had to fend for myself and figure out a way to escape from Boyar Dobre's filthy hands. When the boyar saw my absentminded expression, he turned around and sat on his mini throne.

"What a delectable treat I found. Lady Dobre is at her parents and...," he said as if speaking to himself, but quickly returned his attention to me. "Till the moment we clear up your name, I want you to serve only me and Lady Dobre. She is now mending her health in order to bring a Dobre heir in the future, so your duties will resume to serving me. I will talk with Mama Nica. You will clean my chamber, make my bed, clean my garments. Aren't you happy you won't have to deal with those lowly maids anymore? But do not forget, I want to see how dedicated you are to your cause and my benevolence."

I itched to say I'd rather shovel horse manure alongside Smaranda, than wash his pants for a living, but he didn't even pay attention to my reaction. He simply pushed me out the chamber as if I was cattle and accompanied me back to the kitchen. There we found Mama Nica alone, pouring boiled sour milk in a cloth to make cheese later. She rarely did this herself, but since she probably couldn't go to sleep without finding what would happen to me, Mama Nica found a way to use the time productively.

"Cook Nica, I am here to remove this maid from her kitchen duties."

"This maid's name is Petra," she said, not paying attention to his presence.

"Maid Petra is to be excused from her duties under your authority. She is to serve solely the Dobre family as how the head of the household will deem pertinent."

"Has aging not been kind to you, Boyar Dobre, that you seek special assistance?" Mama Nica asked, placing both hands on her hips.

A short giggle escaped my lips, angering the boyar.

"Cook Nica, let me remind you that you came to ME with the matter in question. This is my way of handling things. You might have authority between these kitchen walls but not in the entire castle. I showed enough grace to be of help to you in your time of need. Being an honorable man, I will excuse your insubordination, but my good nature could change anytime," said the boyar as the air around us thickened.

My heart dropped like a boulder, but Mama Nica remained unwavering. This woman had guts of steel. "I simply did my duty as a keeper of the castle and informed the higher ups about an incident happening between these walls. My actions did not entail you to remove a helpful pair of hands from my kitchen and use them for your personal interests."

The more they debated, the smaller I felt. At one moment, I wished to transform into an ant and run away.

"At the moment, I am the higher authority, thus it is in my power to decide. Further along the way, when His Majesty returns, the decision could be challenged. Until then, the girl stays with me and that is an order." His nostrils flared as if ready to spew fire.

"Let me remind you, Lord Dobre, that no matter who they serve, the maids are to sleep in the servants' quarters. I would assume you understand the consequences of not obeying the law made by the castle's ancestors?"

"It is in my bloodline to obey century old laws and, be assured, Cook Nica, I do not intend on breaking them now or any time soon."

Ignoring the boyar, Mama Nica turned toward me and clutched my hands.

"No matter what happens you will always find a safe place here. You can go to sleep now. Lord Dobre and I must finish our talk."

I nodded and kept my head low, trying to hide my tears. She stepped closer and whispered in my ear, "he might force you to be his maid, but dare he touch even a strand of your hair, I'll make sure he meets his dead mother soon. Don't worry, my child."

I ran to the girls' chamber, but everyone was sleeping by now. How I wished to tell them everything. Pretending to be mute saved me from many dangers, but now it gnawed at me. How I wished I could speak. But nothing could be done. Accepting the sour truth, I decided to go to bed. The whole night, I slept intermittently, waking up from nightmares about my prospects of becoming a consort to a perverted boyar. I didn't even want to be near him, but to sleep with him and to know his wife would hear us from an adjacent room sent agonizing shivers down my spine.

For the next few weeks, I catered to most of Boyar Dobre's needs. He indeed listened to Mama Nica and didn't touch me or hint in the slightest about becoming his consort. Every day I would exit the castle with a sigh of relief and hope that maybe he would change his mind. Some tasks consisted in bringing him a pitcher of wine, or a piece of parchment for a letter he needed to write. Other times, when him and other nobles had a gathering, he would require me to serve them. Then he would deliberately drop a chicken leg on the floor and force me to pick it up. After, he would smirk approvingly and ask me to leave. If Gabriel would've witnessed such a scene, I feared for Boyar Dobre and his companion's livelihoods.

In time, his public games of perverted humiliation increased in consistency and levels. In terms of touching me, he never crossed a line, but the multiple ways he used to his advantage proved how deranged he truly was. The longer time passed, the more satisfied he became with his wicked games. But I kept convincing myself that as long as he didn't place his hands on me, I could manage. That is, till one time he grabbed my breasts from behind and whispered in my ear: "I cannot wait for you to satisfy my every whim in bed. Dare tell Nica and you'll never see the sun rise again."

I realized it was time. The perverted boyar had to be stopped. For sick people it was never enough. The humiliation would continue till I killed him, or he killed me. There had to be a way out of this mess without me having a stake inserted through my navel. But what? What would my sister do? She always had the great ideas.

That night, my eyes stayed open, trying to figure out what to do next. When the girls fell into a deep sleep, I took out my phone and the travel charger from my bag. I plugged it into my phone and, to my surprise I got three precent battery charge out of it. Unfortunately, the phone was of little to no use here. “Eh, where’s the internet when you really need it,” I whispered. The only information I had was in the phone’s notes, but I hardly remembered what I saved. To my surprise, when I scrolled through, I found The Wallachian History textbook and I couldn’t contain my glee. Vlad the Impaler’s rule had three pages of writing, but it was enough for me. I read it several times and an idea came to me. Given the massive risk level, my only question was would I be able to pull it off?

∞ ∞ ∞

On one of my morning visits to the boyar’s chamber, I noticed he left the writing compartment open. Before, I tried many times to look for my pendant but to no avail. Every time he would watch and appraise my every move like a sleazy owl. This time was different. The boyar was still sleeping soundly, and I couldn’t pass on such an opportunity. I tiptoed to the table, took a piece of parchment and a quill, and dipped it in the inkwell. I never used such rudimentary tools to write something, but I wanted to try it. Several times I made ink blobs which spread like spider webs across the paper when I held the quill on the same spot for too long. It took a few more tries to get accustomed to writing this way which felt more like scratching.

Following my morning practice in the art of calligraphy (if one could call it that), I went into the kitchen to fetch Boyar Dobre's breakfast, when Mama Nica stopped and asked me to wait. After all the girls gathered, Mama Nica told us to prepare for today there will be a feast. The *voivode* and his retinue returned from a successful expedition, so we had to prepare a few roosters for the feasting table.

All of a sudden, opposite emotions encompassed me, varying from dread to excitement. I was going to see Gabriel again, but I feared it wouldn't be a pleasant encounter. Maybe he already didn't wish to speak to me, but after finding about me becoming Boyar Dobre's consort he won't wish to see me either.

Shortly after, I got summoned into Boyar Dobre's chamber. He sat at his desk writing something, crossing it, and writing again. For the longest time I stood there in silence while he took care of whatever concerned him. While still looking at the parchment, he spoke, "I prepared an outfit for you. As my future consort, I don't want to present you in these rags to His Majesty." He raised his gaze and pointed with a flabby finger at my outfit. "Your new garment is on the bed. You will wear it tonight. And do something with your hair, it looks like a bird's nest. Bring yourself to a decent state so I have something to show. You are dismissed for now.

CHAPTER 15

That evening I went to the girls' chamber and put on the dress on top of my chemise. The pearlescent green silk cloth felt like feathers to the touch. It's been a long time since my skin touched something so smooth. The square neckline dress had enough of a loose fit to not need a tie in the back, except for the buttons on the embroidered cuff sleeves. Though I had two layers on my body, the silk made me feel half naked, so I wrapped a white woolen shawl around my shoulders. I couldn't go barefooted to the feast, but the perverted boyar forgot to give me a pair of shoes. So I went to Mama Nica in the kitchen in hopes she might have something. All the girls went outside to catch the roosters, and she was the only one to see me. Once Mama Nica noticed me, her mouth gaped, she began coughing, and for the longest time, she couldn't contain her surprise.

"Where did you get this? Is it from Boyar Dobre?" she asked.

I nodded.

"He wants to present you tonight?" Distress flashed in her eyes. "But why are you here?"

I raised the hem of my skirt and showed her my dirty

feet.

"The fool forgot the shoes, huh? But why would you care about them unless you wish to make an impression on...," she said and stopped in her train of thought. Mama Nica peered into my eyes to extract that one bit of information she lacked to confirm her suspicion. "I see. Go to my room. Underneath the bed, you will find a pair of leather shoes. It was a gift from a late *voivode*, but I never wore them. They're yours."

I ran frantically to the servants' quarters once more, hoping the girls were too busy playing catch with the roosters to notice me. Once I entered Mama Nica's room, I looked under the bed and found the black leather shoes. The only problem, they were two sizes too big. At that point, though, there wasn't much of a choice. I took the shoes and ran back to the castle as the sun began setting. I already knew I was late.

As I approached the doors of the Great Hall, while putting on the shoes, I noticed the perverted boyar marching to and fro in a frenzy. When he saw me, he grabbed me by my forearm and whisper-yelled, "where were you? You should've been here before everyone sat at the table."

"*Why did the feast start so early? The food wasn't even ready yet.*"

Boyar Dobre noticed my confusion and said, "we first deal with matters of the voivodeship and the castle, and later, we eat. You are one of the matters. Get in quickly before I order a whip on your back. And what is this abomination doing on your back?" He ripped the shawl off my shoulders and threw it in a dark corner. Then he shoved me through the door, resulting in me having a less-than-elegant entrance. Much to my relief, no one paid much attention to my presence. Boyar Dobre didn't let me relax. He grabbed my arm, walked into the hall, and sat us both at one of the tables. The entire room brimmed with celebratory tones due to the recent successful expedition. In a corner stood three musicians playing a small wooden pipe, a lute, and a drum. The music added to the overall joyful mood.

The two massive tables were aligned parallel and led up to the throne where Vlad the Impaler sat. While waiting our turn to speak, a few boyars exchanged words with Boyar Dobre and didn't hesitate to ogle at me and smirk. Those were the moments I wished to have the power to bang these nobles' heads and teach them a lesson on how to respect women. Alas, I had to use other, more civilized methods. Behind the passing boyars, Mama Nica appeared. I knew she abhorred such manifestation, but she most likely felt something would happen, and she didn't want to miss it. That woman had the intuition of a witch, but I felt somewhat reassured, having a person I knew was on my side. Then I met Gabriel's eyes, and whatever confidence I harbored before flew away like a wild bird. He sat next to his father, Vlad the Impaler's right hand, looking as handsome as ever. At first, I feared his reaction would be of hatred and despise, but he looked like his usual joyous self. On the contrary, he perked up once he noticed me, but when he saw me next to the perverted boyar, he became confused. I wished to possess the ability to send mental messages, but, as things were, he had to go through the same experience as everyone else at the feast.

The commotion slowly settled when Vlad spoke of his expedition, his support in Hungary, and the new laws he planned on implementing to make the land free of thieves and traitors. Then he asked if anyone else wished to speak. Boyar Dobre cleared his voice and, like a sleazy rat, wiggled himself from the table and said, "I would like to have a word, Your Majesty."

"So be it. Come forward, Boyar Dobre," said Vlad the Impaler.

The boyar nudged me to follow him in the middle of the hall. I listened and stood next to him in front of a large crowd of curious eyes. The last place my anxiety would wish to be. Several times I thought of running away, and the only thing keeping me on the spot was my determination to get out of this mess.

"It is my greatest honor to present my consort, Petra," he said, digging an elbow into my ribs forcing me to make a forward motion.

I bit my lip to distract myself from looking at Gabriel and seeing his disappointment.

"Who is she of whom you are speaking?" asked Vlad the Impaler.

"She is but an orphan, Your Majesty. A maid to the castle."

"And why would you stoop so low to acquire a consort?" asked Vlad.

"It is but a matter of the heart, Your Majesty."

He scrutinized the perverted boyar, and then his eyes fell on me. Vlad the Impaler must've noticed my impassive demeanor but chose not to pursue the matter.

"If there are no objections from anyone, I see no issue in

approving such a bond," said Vlad the Impaler.

As he spoke, my gaze only aimed at Gabriel. At first, his glassy eyes turned from stunned to bewilderment and, finally, to anger. I could see something brewing inside him, like a force of nature ready to erupt. The sweet smile I always knew him for was long gone. Gabriel rose to express all he had on his chest, but his father's heavy hand dragged him back into his seat. His father whispered something into his ear and convinced him to cease further action. The sheer pain and despair he showed in his gaze hurt me but, at the same time, freed me. What did I expect? No matter what world I lived in, I had to fend for myself. There were no knights, no shining armor, and no white horses. Just human frailty. And if I wished to survive, I had to take matters into my own hands. Always. It's what my sister taught me. And now was my cue to do precisely that.

"I object, Your Majesty," I said, slowly weighing every word to sound as close to a Wallachian speaker as possible. "This boyar has mistreated a noblewoman."

The gasps rolled across the hall like a wave. Everyone began whispering, "wasn't she mute?", "is she a Saxon?", "her way with words is different." The perverted boyar turned toward me, ready to interject, but the shock silenced him. Stupor took hold of everyone except Mama Nica.

"You say you are of noble roots," continued Vlad Dracula, "but how can you prove it? What I've heard until now are the lies of you being mute. Also, how did a noblewoman enter my palace unnoticed?"

"I am the illegitimate daughter of the late king Albert The Magnanimous. I have been persecuted by my half-brothers and sisters, all of whom did not want me to live. I had to flee in the middle of the night with the help of a trusted servant whom I had lost along the way. I was left alone in an unknown land which I later discovered to be Wallachia. When I took the risk of jumping in a carriage, I realized it went through Your Majesty's castle gates. Afterward, I was blessed to receive help from Mama Nica and her wonderful daughters. And for that, I give her my honorable thank you." I bowed to Mama Nica, who, in return, nodded in appreciation.

The whispers increased like flies buzzing from one mouth to another. I only hoped the numerous nights I spent concocting my plan of action were enough to save my life.

"Why would the daughter of the king of Hungary, albeit a bastard one, decide to stoop so low as to work as a servant in a Wallachian castle when the easiest thing to do was come forward and speak to me?" asked Vlad the Impaler.

"I did not know with which ruler you were in great relations, Sire, thus I preferred to give myself time to learn more about Your Majesty. I am delighted to find Your Majesty's actions embellished by honorable conduct." I wished to tell him more about how much of a fan I was, but I couldn't risk it.

"It is wise for anyone to flatter their superior, especially one who could ensure capital punishment at the snap of a finger. Thus, your words bring me more doubt than reassurance," said Vlad.

"I have proof, Sire. I arrived here with a pendant in the shape of a four-leaf clover with a red jewel as a center. The jewel has been discovered by one of my Wallachian sisters here and had been presented to Mama Nica. Afterward,

Boyar Dobre took the jewel and reassured me he would present it today in front of His Majesty. It is the proof of my noble roots."

The perverted boyar kept silent for a second, glanced at me in disgust, then returned his gaze to Vlad the Impaler, and said, "I do not know of what jewel this servant speaks of. She is but an orphan and has been, for a short time, a maid to the castle. Whatever she's trying to show here are lies to persuade Your Majesty to alter her status in the castle. As if being a consort of a boyar is not enough."

"I understand Boyar Dobre's unwillingness to admit in hiding something that is mine," I said. "I will have no choice but to prove my noble roots and pertinence to a royal family another way. I will require a piece of parchment and a quill."

Another wave of surprised reactions moved along the crowd. As everyone waited for the required materials, I clasped my hands in front and lowered my head. With my peripheral vision, I could see the drops of sweat rolling from Boyar Dobre's forehead. I felt his body trembling with anger when he came closer to me and whispered, "what are you trying to prove, wench? Wait till we get out of here. The whip is itching for you."

I chose not to look in his direction or react to his words. I chose instead to stand my ground firmly. When the parchment and quill arrived and were handed to me, I walked to the table where Mama Nica sat. I needed a boost of confidence, and her gaze gave me just that. I wrote slowly, careful to not leave blobs of ink on the entire paper while tens of eyes glared at my every move. Afterward, I stepped toward Vlad the Impaler and gave him the parchment. He read it, smiled (the first I'd ever seen him do so), and then presented it to the crowd. I imagined few could read, but everyone could see clearly. Something was written on that parchment, and it said: "Vlad Draculya est Walachia *voivode*." It was written in Latin and said he was Wallachia's ruler.

Boyar Dobre took a few steps backward and sat on a chair next to Mama Nica's table. Gabriel, as well as his father, leaned closer to their ruler in order to see the words I wrote on the parchment. It was rare for a man to know how to write, but for a woman, it was outright preposterous.

"Since when can a woman write? It is unheard of." Vlad Dracula's demeanor changed suddenly.

I couldn't help but feel flattered by the words of my hero. "Well, I had lived close to the kingdom and learned from…"

"You must be a witch," said Vlad, visibly infuriated and pointing at me.

To my dismay, my plan took an unexpected turn.

CHAPTER 16

"I have learned from a tutor sent by my father. I know how to write not many words but enough to prove my royal roots."

Vlad the Impaler hesitated maybe for a second but remained suspicious. In one last attempt, I ran to the musicians' corner. The musicians were oblivious to what was happening and didn't mind me borrowing their pipe. I had years of practice playing the recorder, but that happened many years ago. I hoped my fingers won't clam up and I would find enough air in my lungs to produce a sound. I began wiping the pipe with the sleeve of my dress to give myself more time and try to figure out what to play. I only remembered Three Blind Mice, so I said: "I will play a tragic ballad about the same past meant to become our future." I played the melody slowly and with as much emotion as I could muster. The stunned looks on their faces told me everything. A lady in the back even said, "what a touching melody, indeed."

After I finished my performance, everyone clapped.

"You are indeed a noblewoman to be able to perform so well," said Vlad the Impaler.

"I'm flattered by your kind words, Your Majesty," I

curtsied in the clumsiest way possible, but it didn't matter. They already bought my story.

"You will receive an official invitation to stay at my palace. You will be called a princess in this voivodeship and addressed as Milady. I disapprove of the liaison between you and Boyar Dobre, for it is beneath your status to become a consort. However, given your Hungarian origin, you will be held as a royal hostage, similar to how I spent my youth in The Ottoman Empire. You will be granted all commodities in the castle, but you are not allowed to leave. As long as you reside under my roof, you will be granted protection. But remember, I trust only those who prove my trust. If you betray me and the Wallachian voivodeship, you will be executed."

"So be it, Your Majesty," I said and curtsied again, this time more elegantly.

"Now we will feast," said Vlad the Impaler. "Mama Nica, please order your girls to bring food, as it seems our appetites have grown wild. Boyar Dobre, please take a seat at your table. Milady, you will sit next to me."

I joined my hero at the dinner table, and being so close, I could feel the overarching power this man exuded. I felt protected by a fatherly figure, though he wasn't as old as it seemed. It felt unusual that, for the first time, I wasn't the one putting plates on the table. When the girls saw me sitting next to their ruler, they looked dumbfounded. Several times they glanced at me and then at Mama Nica. The elderly woman approached the girls fearing they would drop the plates and explained in a few words what had happened. A sense of guilt took over me. A few hours ago, we were sisters who worked shoulder to shoulder, sharing the same unjust fate, and now they had to serve me. Who knows? Maybe Smaranda (or any of them) was indeed a Saxon or Hungarian Princess. The only difference between their provenience and mine was that I forged my royal roots with the help of technology they couldn't yet comprehend.

After dinner, the nobles gathered in small groups to drink some wine and discuss all relevant topics from that week (most likely about me) while the girls cleaned the tables. Boyar Dobre left as soon as the feast ended. I opened a discussion with a few ladies who expressed wonderment from witnessing such an erudite noblewoman. And as we spoke, I felt a lingering shadow behind me. When I turned, it was Gabriel watching me like a hawk while pretending to listen to his father speak. I could see how tight he held to his volition not to approach me. "*It is what you deserve.*" I turned back to the ladies and asked to be excused. Then, I went to Mama Nica and asked her to show me the way to my chamber. I wished to be done with the night as soon as possible.

Mama Nica explained where my future living conditions would be and went to grab some linen for my bed while I walked in the opposite direction toward the nobles' chambers. The night descended so deep into the corners of the castle the torches were incapable of illuminating them. As I distanced myself further from the Great Hall, silence settled between the crevices of the walls. If the atmosphere wasn't eerie enough, I began hearing heavy steps coming my way. I feared Boyar Dobre was drawing near to take revenge upon me, so I increased the speed of my steps. Unfortunately, the other person's presence loomed closer behind, no matter how fast I ran. I went with plan B and hid behind a poorly illuminated arched wall. The only problem was I couldn't see anything and could calculate the distance of the incoming steps by their loudness. I stayed in the dark, inhaling musty and moldy dread till the steps stopped. "*Maybe it was a random boyar who just entered his chamber*," I thought. When I peeked for a second, the apparition stood right before me. I screamed as loud as my lungs could handle and sprinted out of there. But the apparition was faster. It locked a hand around my arm, pulled me toward its chest, and enveloped me in an embrace from behind. I fought to free myself till it whispered in my ear, "it's me, Gabriel."

I relaxed like an overcooked noodle, exhausted from all the chaos in my brain. We stood motionless behind the arched wall for quite a while, trying to compensate for all the missed time. He didn't tell me explicitly he missed me, but every fiber of my body felt how much he and maybe I yearned for each other's presence. But I knew we couldn't remain like this forever, so I let myself revel in his closeness for a bit longer. It was hard to admit, but I missed the sweet scoundrel. But it had to stop. There were too many things for me to take care of, and falling in love wasn't included in the Forged Wallachian Princess To Do list. It could actually hinder my chances of finding a way to return home, especially after today's events. The fantasy they spoon-fed us as kids, of knights in shining armor, of damsels in distress, blah, blah, blah, all one big pile of bogus. Knights were humans like the rest of us, and damsels could fend for themselves. Thank you very much. I would've ranted in my head longer if he hadn't spun me around. The moment I saw the outline of his face and body,

I froze. He was indeed a very handsome man. Too bad he lived in the wrong time period.

"Are you indeed a princess?" he whispered in my ear.

"Are you truthfully a knight?" I asked, trying to hurt him as much as he did me.

"I had to act this way upon my father's request," he said in a pained tone.

"From what I understand, you are old enough to be your own man."

"Not when you're the son of His Majesty's second in command."

"Thus, your father's decisions are your decisions."

"I am here of my own volition."

"Yes, hiding behind a wall in the darkness. It is not the kind of entanglement I wish to involve myself in."

"I hope my actions today didn't mislead you to think I had ill intentions before."

"No, but it convinced me you didn't have serious intentions."

"I beg to differ. What happened had nothing to do with how serious I am about us and everything to do with my family. As a knight in His Majesty's retinue, there are duties I must fulfill and loyalty I must prove to my family. It is the honor of a knight."

"What happened to your knight's honor tonight? The one time I needed you to stand up for me, you failed. How can you imagine me trusting you not to do the same next time?" I ripped myself from his embrace.

"The circumstance took me by surprise. The last time we met, I shared a kiss with a feisty hazel-eyed maid. Today I stand before a feisty Milady. But in my heart, I care about Petra, who trusted me to take her out of the forest in her most vulnerable state. I care about Petra, who secretly helps Mama Nica with her sewing because the old woman is losing her sight. I care about Petra, who has a heart of gold but will never admit it.

"My father wasn't the only reason I sat back. I had to avoid making rash decisions. In such matters, it could be a threshold between life and death. But you must understand, even if Boyar Dobre would've made you his consort tonight, I could still claim you as a wife tomorrow. Today's path didn't lead to an end, but I was impressed by the continuity you gave it."

"Are all knights such sweet talkers, or only you? I've been burnt too many times to trust spoken words. Your actions will prove your intentions. Nothing else. In the meantime, I must excuse myself, for I need to move into my new living conditions," I said and turned around to leave.

He grabbed me by my hand once more, though I didn't turn, and said, "if action is what you need. Action is what you will get." Gabriel let go of my hand, turned around, and walked the other way.

I stood in one place, listening to his footsteps. Each step felt like a jab in my heart. I wished to believe him, but after the loss of my sister and Elijah's betrayal, there was no way I could find enough power to mend my heart a third time. Eventually, I commenced my walk, but once I got closer to my chamber door, I realized I had to retrieve my bag from the servants' quarters tonight. Who knows what Smaranda would do if she found everything stashed in it?

I walked back, hoping to avoid any encounters along the

way. To my dismay, a flock of nobles walked in my direction, and I had no place to hide in sight. Once the distance between us shortened, every boyar and their wife presented themselves and expressed their honor of meeting the daughter of Albert the Magnanimous. In my usual polite way, I thanked them, which baffled the crowd since superiors never showed gratitude toward anyone beneath their rank. Well, they were in luck today. I excused myself and walked away, parading my most modelesque strut. It wasn't clear if it worked, but I heard a few gasps from behind.

I entered the servants' quarters, hoping the girls would be fast asleep and I could go in and out in incognito mode. As I opened the girls' chamber door, I realized how wrong I was in my assumption.

The girls sat somberly around a candlelight, drinking from a wine bottle.

"Oh, ye look who's here. If it ain't the great princess Petra the Mag- Magnanimous," said Smaranda tripping on her words.

CHAPTER 17

"Keep your mouth shut, Smaranda, or you're going to get us all in trouble," said Anca.

I decided to ignore them and simply took my day attire, night chemise, and the bag folded in a scarf and headed toward the door.

"Is it true you are leaving us?" asked Lia, trying to cover her tears with her pigtails.

The question stopped me in my tracks. Even if Smaranda and I had bad blood, the other girls didn't deserve to be treated the same way. I turned around, placed my things on my bed, made sure to place the bag underneath the clothes, and sat next to Teodora. In the flickering light of the candle, the girls looked distraught. With all the conundrum that happened earlier, I forgot they deserved an explanation. But before I could explain myself, Smaranda got in my way. "So, are you a Saxon princess like I said I was, or something new like a Hungarian princess?"

"At the moment, I am a Wallachian princess and would appreciate you treating me like one."

"You're nothing but a liar. I knew you could speak, and I'm still questioning if you're a *strigoaică*, but a princess?

Pfft." Smaranda shook her head and looked at me with an inebriated scowl.

"It is not for you to decide who I am. Only His Majesty's decision can be final," I said.

"Look at her speaking so well. As if she's been speaking her entire life," Smaranda said.

"Quit it, Smaranda. It is enough," said Anca, exasperated. Smaranda looked at her with half-opened eyes and went back to drinking wine straight from the bottle.

"I realize the distress I caused you but rest assured Petra from before didn't go anywhere. I am still the same person who didn't know how to carry two buckets of water at the same time, how to knead dough, or milk goats and cows. Remember the time each squeeze I made went straight into my eye? I'm glad to see you laugh now at my misgivings, but then I was grateful you gave me a helping hand. You have earned my deepest respect, and my warm feelings for you will never change. Even if I begin a new life at the castle, my heart will be here with you. And no, you will not get some preposterous request like gathering field flowers for Lady Dobre's bath."

They all laughed, except for Smaranda.

"Anca, you are such a strong woman. I wish to learn your ways. Lia, you are still young to see the games happening in the castle, and I hope you never get to experience them. Teodora, I have wanted to tell you for a long time: you are a sweet, beautiful young woman who deserves a bright future ahead. I only request you to avoid the flower fields, and everything will be fine. And lastly, Smaranda, I never intended for you to hate me, and I wish to stop this quarrel as soon as you let me. A truce is far better than a never-ending war."

Smaranda mumbled something underneath her nose but withheld any snarky comment. I hugged each of the girls. Smaranda refused. I took my belongings and left.

I rushed through the castle halls, knowing very well Mama Nica was waiting for me. The lady needed her sleep, and I kept her awake in the middle of the night. When I reached the door, I was huffing and puffing like an exhausted train.

"Does Milady need any more help from your humble servant?" she asked, sarcasm dripping from her words.

I took a few more large breaths before I could answer. "Mama Nica, you and the girls are leading the same teasing game. I am the same Petra you've always known. Nothing changes just because I live in the castle now, and I hope you'll still regard me as one of your daughters."

"Oh, life is just one change after another, dearie." She came closer and caressed my cheek. "But you will always be my daughter, and as my daughter, I wish you would've told me sooner. Maybe then you wouldn't have had to deal with Boyar Dobre."

"All happened for the better."

"Indeed so," Mama Nica said and became pensive. Then she spoke, "From now on, I will address you as Milady, and your request will be my command. Don't you dare come to the kitchen unless to request something, am I clear? Do not disrespect His Majesty by acting like a servant."

"Yes, Mama Nica. I'll do as you say."

She hugged me like a mother sending her daughter out into the world. "In this case, I must request a cup of milk and bread each morning. At least you'll have less work with me," I said, smiling, but she slapped me on the back.

"What did I just say? Milk and bread are for servants. You will get at least a slice of cheese. Come, let me show you to your new chamber. Before, though, hold this linen so I can open the door."

Just when I began feeling like a noble, Mama Nica reminded me very fast who was the boss in this castle. Some things or people never changed. But it was what I loved most about her. After she handed me the white linen, she took the candle held in her other hand and lit it from the closest torch. Then she fished a rusty key the size of her palm from her embroidered belt and began unlocking the door. As she fiddled with the lock, I realized while Vlad the Impaler's chamber was at the far end of the hall, Gabriel's chamber was quite close to mine. "*Great. Now it will be even harder to avoid him,*" I thought.

When we entered my new lodging, we were met with a cold room lit only by a narrow beam of light from the window. A large four-poster bed, covered with a quilt sewn in a Turkish style rather than Wallachian, and a wooden trunk at its end. Vlad had definitely been exchanging gifts with The Ottoman sultan. The rugs beside the bed were made in a traditional Wallachian style, with a black background and vivid red and pink flowers. Up in one corner hung a small icon of St. Andrews. Underneath the icon stood a table and chair similar to Boyar Dobre's chamber.

"This chamber has a fireplace. I don't know why His Majesty decided to build one. A furnace would've heated up the room in haste. They learn things from outside and try to make the Wallachian lands like they belong there when we have beauty hiding here on every corner."

It was hard to compare it to anything else but a museum room like the ones in Bran castle. It felt cold, moldy, and uninviting. My room in Seattle felt ten times more welcoming than this cold beauty. But let's be honest, given my previous arrangement, it exceeded all expectations.

Mama Nica started the fire while I made the bed.

"Last time I let you help, young lady," she said while shoving more wood with a poker.

I smiled but didn't respond.

"Don't tell you've gone mute again."

"I was never mute. I just came from far away."

"Well, now you're a princess here. It is all that matters," Mama Nica said and began coughing.

"Are you well?" I asked.

"Yes, the ash makes my cough worse."

"Have you talked to the castle doctor?"

"He's more of a cattle doctor. And the last thing I want is to be treated like a cow."

"You should try to put some mint leaves in hot water. It could help ease the pain."

"We thought it peculiar when you used cherry leaves. Now you want me to try mint?"

"It will do no harm. Of that, I'm sure. Well, unless you're allergic."

"Allergic? What does it mean?" Mama Nica rose to face me.

"It's when your body doesn't like something, and it can make you sneeze, itch, or swell. It's what Teodora has. You should not send her to the flower field. It will make her feel better."

"Where did you find such knowledge?" she asked, perplexed.

"My father's doctor."

"Why these Hungarian doctors know everything in this world."

"Well…"

"Enough for today. Please have a good rest, Milady. Tomorrow I will ask for finer chemises. For now, please accept the one you had before," she said and waddled to the door.

"I don't believe chemises peel off the skin once it is found their owner is of noble roots, but thank you, Mama Nica."

"This room hasn't been heated well since last winter, and it is autumn already. If you want to—"

"I'm good, Mama Nica. I'm used to the cold. Go get some rest. It's been a long day."

She nodded and closed the door after herself.

And, for the first time since I time traveled, I found myself alone. Alone with my thoughts, worries, and realizations. I collapsed on the floor and sobbed. I mourned my previous life, my parents, Mei, and my school. My parents probably thought I was dead by now.

"Oh no. They probably already realized I had disappeared. Just like my sister," I said.

I wonder how they were dealing with the news. When my sister disappeared, they were barely coping with day-to-day tasks. But to lose two daughters and not know how will destroy them. How I wished to tell them I was alive and well. I hoped they didn't do anything rash. The tears began flowing down my cheeks. "Get it together, Petra. Wipe away these tears and focus. If there was a way to travel to this place, there must be a way back."

I had to find a way to get home. As much as I liked the people from this time period, I couldn't renounce my previous life. The first thing I had to do was retrieve the pendant. This whole mess started with it, so everything had to end with it. It was clear that Boyar Dobre wouldn't simply give it back. I had to figure out a more extensive plan and maybe gather information from the girls. Anca could be a good person to talk to, but would she risk her life for someone who lied to her extensively? Gabriel was out of the question. I couldn't trust him. Plus, any question regarding the boyar could cause a massive altercation between the two, and I didn't want to bring more attention to this situation. The less I got noticed by the nobles, the more they could focus on their internal and external political affairs and I on mine. Also, even if his words earlier were honest, I didn't want to give Gabriel any hope if I planned on returning. I couldn't risk it. He had to focus on his life. I didn't want to ruin his marriage prospects, as it was one of the most important aspects of a person's life during the medieval period.

Interestingly, since I knew how history would unfold, could I help them? I didn't get the chance to apply any significant changes that could alter the future. Yet. Then again, I had to be careful though. Who knows how the butterfly effect could change the entire European history, if not the whole world's. But for now, greater things had to be postponed as my eyelids seemed to not listen to my brain and close on their own. I rushed to put on my night chemise and snuggle in the large bed. No hay pillows in sight. Only feathers of the best quality. My head dipped into one as if into butter. The quilt felt to be of superior quality as well. Though the night became colder and colder, and I could hear the wind howling at the window, the warmth of the quilt covering my body enveloped me and whisked me into a world of dreams.

During the night, I had what felt like a lucid dream. At first, I heard a creak in the window. I thought it was the wind and didn't pay any attention. Then before I realized it, I found myself in the embrace of a winged man.

CHAPTER 18

He had a long, chiseled face, translucent skin, bright golden hair, green cat-like eyes, and white wings spreading out from his back. If nothing else, he looked like a real angel. I wanted to ask what he was doing in my dream, but he simply smiled and began trailing kisses on my neck and shoulders. When he raised his head to kiss my lips, I refused and turned away. But he caressed my chin slowly and brought it back to face him. As I looked into his eyes, I realized the only one I wished for was him. He kissed me voraciously and began untying the knot at the top of my chemise. I began fidgeting and accidentally bit his lip. That woke me from the dream. It was already morning. I looked around, but no one was there.

Except for the fluttering noise the wind made as it escaped through a crack in the window. The windows in this building didn't open. With an arched and narrow shape, their only purpose was to bring light into the dimly lit castle. Though my room's window had an unintentional opening, no grown man or child could step through the narrow arch. Plus, on the outside, besides the piles of sharp stakes and moats surrounding the area, the tall and steep build of the castle purposively made it extremely difficult to climb it. I assumed whatever I saw during the night had to be a dream stemming from all the events that happened yesterday. As I wondered, someone knocked at the door, startling me.

"Um… Come in?"

Anca entered with a breakfast tray which consisted of a boiled egg, a piece of bread, and cheese. She was one of the few humans I wished to see this morning. Then like we usually did as maids, she excused herself without even glancing at me and attempted to exit the chamber.

"Anca, I hope your opinion of me didn't worsen after the night's sleep."

"You are a guest of His Majesty. Your presence will be held with the utmost honor."

"I'm still the same Petra as you always knew. Whatever happens, you should know I'll be on your side."

"Thank you, Milady. It is an honor to be in Milady's regard."

"I have another question. What does a Milady do during the day?"

She looked at me with a confounded expression.

"I meant to say what a lady does in a Wallachian castle. Every castle is different." I smiled to cover my lie.

"Some ladies prefer to walk in the garden, others pray in church, but most gather in Lady Codreanu's chamber and sew. It is up to the ladies to decide how they should spend their day."

"I suppose today I should visit the gardens," I said.

"As you wish, Milady," she said, bowed, and walked out of the chamber.

The day went by fast, as most of it was spent on me recovering from the past months of work. The gardens didn't have much to show as autumn took away all the blooms. Still, I enjoyed the walk while I met other ladies and boyars along my path. Several times I itched to visit Mama Nica in the kitchen, but I feared she would smack me on the back and send me on my "noble" merry way. I didn't realize how boring it was for these noble women. Besides birthing babies and walks, nothing much could be done. I hated to admit it but tending to Vincenta van Goat's needs proved far more fulfilling than I expected.

At noon, as I walked through the castle halls, I heard giggles from a chamber. When I got closer, a lady opened the door and said, "let me ask in the kitchen. Maybe Mama Nica has more needles."

"*Needles and threads? That's my jam*," I thought and peeked inside. In the room were five ladies sewing, knitting, and chitchatting. "*It must be Lady Codreanu's sewing club Anca told me about*."

"Oh, Princess Petra, come in. Join us," said Lady Codreanu. She wore a long-sleeved silk brown dress with pearls attached at the neckline.

"I was just passing by," I said as she interlaced her arm around mine and pulled me in.

"We were all talking about yesterday's events. Where did you learn to play the pipe so exquisitely?" asked Lady Codreanu.

"I learned from a world-renowned music tutor, Sir Garcia," I said, remembering my orchestra teacher in elementary school. The entire school district knew him, which was famous enough for me.

"I wish I would've known his name before," said Lady Codreanu as the other four ladies nodded.

"He's more famous in the West." It was more like West West and in about five hundred years in the future.

"You don't say. How fascinating. Can you sew?" she asked as she sat on her cushioned chair.

"Yes, I can." Excitement began rising in me. I missed cross-stitching and embroidering so much. Mama Nica would only let me mend linen and shirts.

"Today, we are embroidering flowers on tablecloths for Lady Munteanu. Her wedding is coming soon," Lady Codreanu said and gave me an embroidery hoop with the tablecloth runner already attached to it.

"I'm knitting her a shawl for winter as a wedding gift," said one of the other ladies.

"This is the pattern we follow," she presented me with a finished version of the flower. It wouldn't be enough for a novice to figure out how to do it, but I had it in the bag.

As we settled in our chairs, focusing on the task at hand, they didn't try to pry more information from me. Things in the medieval period changed so fast people had to adapt, and as long as I didn't represent a threat to them, they accepted me living amongst them. After a good amount of silent work and a laugh here and there at innocuous matters, we heard the door creak. It was Lady Dobre entering the room with her own embroidery hoop. The air suddenly turned cold. All the ladies glared at her for a second and then returned to their tasks as if a ghost had appeared and disappeared in a matter of seconds. I supposed the entire Dobre family had to suffer repercussions because of the perverted head of the household. Lady Dobre didn't show any distress from the attitude her peers displayed. She simply marched toward me and said, "I ask for your forgiveness, Milady, for my husband has treated you with utmost disrespect." She bowed, glace at her peers furtively, then looked at me in despair. She pleaded silently for me to accept her apology so she could regain the graces of her companions. Lady Dobre might've been a bitter person, but I had Mama Nica and my girls, at least, while she had these ladies who scorned her the moment her reputation got tarnished. As if she could control that fool of a husband.

"I grant you forgiveness, Lady Dobre," I said as gasps spread across the room. To show I meant it, I rose from the chair and shook her hand, to which she reciprocated with excitement.

"Lady Dobre, don't just stand there. Come take a sit next to me," said Lady Codreanu.

Lady Dobre nodded and did as requested.

With some peace restored, we continued our needlework, but as quietude settled between us, I remembered my dream. The incessant reappearance of the angel in my mind didn't let me relax. But if I mentioned this dream to anyone, my reputation as a newly forged princess could be tainted with rumors. Men climbing through maiden's windows at night did not sound great even as a dream. If there could be such a man who could climb a steep wall with their bare hands and fit through the narrow window. No, this was an issue to be discussed only with the correct type of people.

I took it as a mission to finish the flower as soon as possible and leave. I had to find some answers before the night settled.

"Princess Petra, your sewing mastery is impressive," Lady Codreanu said as I handed her my work. "Please do join us tomorrow as well."

"It will be an honor, Lady Codreanu. But, I must depart at the moment due to other matters."

They all rose and bowed to me. I almost bowed to them but stopped myself in time. This etiquette thing took so much practice.

When I entered the kitchen, I found Mama Nica all red from the steam of boiling water.

"What are you doing here, Milady?" she asked, surprised. "I asked you to come to the kitchen only for requests."

"But I do have a request, Mama Nica. I must speak to you about a serious issue," I said, and all the girls in the kitchen perked up their ears.

"It is best to speak in my room," she said as she glared at the girls, who immediately returned to their work.

Mama Nica's room remained the same organized mess as last time. Talk about a shoemaker without shoes.

"Sit, sit. Move the yarn from the bed and take a seat. Now, what bothers you, dearie?" Mama Nica always called me dearie when no one was around, and it always warmed my heart.

"Are the windows in the castle supposed to open?"

"No, not from what I heard of."

"When you said, His Majesty built a fireplace in my chamber. Maybe he built a window that could be opened?"

"No, His Majesty would never do so, as it is a safety threat. But what are you trying to say?"

"Well...you see... I had a dream last night."

"A dream?"

"Yes, about an angel."

"To be visited by an angel is such a blessing."

"Well, yes. That is true, but you see...he began kissing me."

"Kissing you? In the dream?"

"Yes, I believe he could be called a naughty angel."

"Naughty? What does it mean?"

"Um, with less than honorable intentions."

"I see. But it was only a dream?"

"Yes, no night visitor entered my room."

"I see. Then I do have to ask you one favor. Leave your chamber's door open this coming night."

"Open?" I asked, surprised. "I expected you to tell me the opposite."

"If it's only a dream, it would not matter. And tomorrow, I'll send one of the servant men to repair the broken window."

"I suppose you are correct. So be it. I will leave the door open per your request. I appreciate it," I said, happy she didn't judge me for having sexy dreams.

The rest of the day went uneventful as if yesterday's events were but a distant memory. At night, Anca brought two dresses, a pair of shoes, and several night chemises, saying they were a gift from the ladies of the castle. I also received a golden ring, a pearl necklace, and long gold earrings. The gifts baffled me, but in no way could I refuse. I asked Anca to place them on the bed. She did so, then excused herself and left. But I couldn't simply go to sleep. I had to play dress up with all this new stuff. I felt like a kid again, trying my mother's dresses.

In the end, tiredness took over me, so I folded my dresses neatly, placed them in the trunk at the end of the bed, and put on my cotton nightgown. It had so much embroidery sewn in it, I could admire the intricated patterns across the fabric all night. Sleep had a different idea. I enjoyed my beauty sleep like any other swindling princess, but, to my dismay, the previous night's dream came back to haunt me.

CHAPTER 19

Like a firefly, he emanated so much sparkle it illuminated the entire room. The light exploded from a tiny speck flying through the crack of the window and transformed into an angel. I could barely deduce his face from all the bright sparkles, but when I did, it mesmerized me. It was impossible to take my eyes off him. He walked closer, or better said levitated, and lay next to me. Up close, his face shined with the power of the entire night sky.

"Did you miss me?" he asked in the most alluring voice.

I was so entranced by his voice I couldn't answer. He pulled me closer to face him and began touching my cheeks, neck, and lips, and said: "I missed you too. I finally have found you." It felt like I was melting in his embrace. Then he began kissing me. Not as good as Gabriel, but so much more irresistible. I didn't want it to stop. The deeper the kiss, the more light he emanated, but for me, it felt draining. As if his kisses sucked all my energy, leaving me so weak, I couldn't hold my head up. At a certain point, my hands fell limp around his neck. He hugged and caressed my hair as he continued to kiss me. The dream felt very real. His touch felt burning hot. When he lay on top of me,

I felt his weight and realized it wasn't a dream. One could not feel a physical change in a dream. He was real, and he indeed had not-so-honorable intentions. At that moment, I thought of Gabriel and what he would think if he saw me like this. How disappointed he would be.

I tried moving my head to break the kiss but to no avail. As a last resort, I screamed through my lips. As usual, no one heard me. The apparition smirked again and pushed his mouth deeper into mine, forcing me to succumb to his charms.

"Do you wish to continue the pleasureful act?" he asked, beaming a smile. "Please say yes."

"Yes, yes," I said, but I didn't know why I said it.

A knock on the door followed, then someone called my name. I ripped my lips from the apparition and turned my head toward the opening door. With hazy eyes, I saw Gabriel. Depleted of all my energy, the only thing I could muster before fainting were the words: "You're here."

∞ ∞ ∞

The thuds inside my head forced me to open my eyes. The night had already settled. When I searched for someone, the person I saw by candlelight wasn't Gabriel but Mama Nica. She kept fervently praying at the edge of my bed.

"Mama Nica…" I said.

"You've woken up," she said in relief.

"What happened?"

"It was Zburătorul."

"Who?"

"It's an unnatural being that charms unmarried maidens

at night. It drains them of their life manna," she said somberly.

"But why did it choose me?"

"It usually happens to those who yearn for a loved one but cannot be with them. It's said that Zburătorul was once a human who loved a maiden dearly. But she died before they could get married. In his grief, he chose to give himself to the devil and become an unnatural being forever searching for his beloved. With the power to fly from window to window, he seeks someone who looks like his loved one, and when he finds her, he uses his magic powers to enchant the maiden. Sometimes, the maiden succumbs to the spell and gifts her honor to the being."

"Honor, huh?" I said, blushing at the memory of yesterday's events. He didn't have to ask too many times for my honor. How could I look into Gabriel's eyes after my disgraceful moans?

"Wait, but how did Gabriel know the being would be there, and how could he know I left the door unlocked?"

The corner of her mouth rose in a somewhat sad smile. "I saw how Gabriel looked at you, so I assumed he would do everything in his power to protect you."

The man really took his promise to heart. "How did he fight Zburătorul?"

"Unnatural beings never fight humans."

"Why?"

"These two worlds are never meant to meet. The good spirits almost always stay in The Other Realm. The bad ones venture into our world to cause havoc, but except for Zburătorul, most unnatural beings attack people who have been touched by magic."

Mama Nica had opened Pandora's box of new information. Why didn't I know any of this before? And I had lived in this godforsaken place for half a year now. The only thing I got used to hearing was Smaranda calling me a *strigoaică*, but no one had mentioned the Flyer, which was how Zburătorul was translated. Yep, he definitely was not an angel.

"Will he leave me alone after Gabriel saved me?"

"Regrettably, no. The only way to escape him is to know the banishing spell or find someone to marry."

"What?" My whole world came crashing down.

"You have awoken, Milady." A deeper voice resounded in the chamber. "How are you feeling?" Gabriel came closer to the bed and took my hand in his.

"I feel better," I said, trying to show my appreciation through my gaze.

Being the wise lady that she was, Mama Nica decided to give us some privacy and excused herself. After she left, Gabriel kneeled at the edge of the bed, examined my face to see if anything was wrong, and then said, "when I heard your voice behind the door, my blood boiled with anger while my heart tightened from fear."

I blushed from embarrassment, remembering, once more, the moans I so eagerly voiced. "They weren't exactly sounds of pain." I looked at my hands.

"Do not be deceived. Whatever you thought you felt was nothing more than a charming spell. You could've fallen asleep never to wake up again."

Indeed, the Flyer took killer charms to a whole new level.

"I can see your hands are warming up. Earlier this

morning, your hands were colder than ice." His voice trembled.

I could see, hear, and feel he cared for me.

"Are you able to get up and walk?" Gabriel asked.

"*What a weird question to ask*," I thought. "I can try," I said.

He gave me his hand for support and helped me get out of bed, but my legs failed me, and I found myself falling into his embrace. I didn't want to admit it, but recently it became my favorite place to be.

"You are still weak," he said with sadness in his voice and laid me back in bed. "You must rest. I will face the lords myself."

"Face the lords?" I asked, but he was already gone.

Mama Nica entered and asked, "How are you feeling, dearie?"

"Why does Gabriel need to face the lords?" I asked.

"I thought Gabriel told you."

"Tell me what?" I raised myself and propped my back on the headboard.

"An unnatural being coming each night to the castle could threaten everyone here. They are having a round table to decide what to do next."

"Say what? They are deciding my fate right now?" I climbed out of bed.

"You might not know it, but good news could come out of this."

"Don't you think I must be present if my fate is being decided?"

"It is not a woman's place to be at the round table with men. It is all in the hands of the All Mighty. We can only pray."

"Gabriel wanted me to go with him."

"Then he would risk angering the higher-ups. You must understand the danger of being chosen by unnatural beings, Milady," she said, trying to suppress a cough.

Mama Nica never behaved in such a defeated manner. Either she knew more than she wanted to say, or the fear of the unknown kept her from fighting.

"I have to go," I said.

"You are weak, my dear."

"No, I'm not," I said and got up. Without Gabriel's support, the walls began spinning, and I almost fell to the ground.

"Take it easy. And where are you going only in your underdress? At least get dressed."

"Give me whatever you can find, for I will not stop."

"Here." She took a dress from the trunk. Mama Nica helped me put it on as I tried my best not to fall. It was one of the newest dresses gifted by the ladies of the castle. If nothing else, I would at least look presentable as I fought for my future.

I wobbled through the chamber's door, grasping its frame for the much-needed support. Mama Nica didn't walk me to the hall as I impetuously asked her not to. I put on a brave face and walked with my head high out of my chamber, but the moment I closed the door and got in the hallway, I curled up like a question mark and was forced to take small steps toward the Great Hall. I walked and then took a breather, then walked some more and took a longer breather. When a noblewoman walked by, I straightened my back and pretended I took a leisurely stroll, but once she was out of sight, I reverted to my curled-up state.

When I reached the hall, I heard male voices arguing. I rushed through the large doors, and right when I felt my weak legs betray me again, a pair of strong arms enveloped me in their embrace. I raised my gaze and saw Gabriel. Given the many times he had caught me, I had to call him my personal safety net. For a moment, it felt like we were the only people in the room.

Only when he brought me back to my feet, I realized the number of men gathered. At least twenty boyars encompassed my gaze, including Boyar Dobre and Vlad the Impaler as a center point. The amount of scowling stares made me lean closer toward Gabriel.

"Glad you could join us, Milady," Vlad said, but his tone implied I wasn't supposed to be there.

"I learned that my fate was to be decided tonight. Thus, I considered my presence an obligatory matter," I said, distancing myself from Gabriel's supporting arm around my back.

Every boyar there made different disapproving movements, from head shakes to "tsks" and furtive looks toward their ruler. Vlad, compared to the boyars, gave a heartful laugh.

"A woman's place is not at the round table, but I will accept the disobedience one last time, given you are a guest in my castle. I have already lost precious time deciding what to do with this issue. The country is facing a harsh winter ahead, but I'm here saving the castle from a dreadful creature brought in by you, Milady. But if you mutter one word without being asked, do fear my wrath, Princess," he said and watched me like a hawk to see if I obeyed his order.

I nodded bashfully, leaning into Gabriel like a puppy with her tail between her legs.

"Now," Vlad the Impaler continued, "what are we to do with our guest, my lords?"

"As I said before, Your Majesty, the best way to deal with unnatural occurrences tied to a human is to banish the human," said Gabriel's father and second in command.

I glanced at Gabriel, who had a wry expression but overall remained unperturbed.

"And where do you expect us to banish her, Lord Stoica?" asked Vlad the Impaler.

"Out of Wallachian lands," Lord Stoica answered sheepishly.

"Where do you offer to send her? Back to the Hungarian kingdom? If her usurpers find out, they will use her against us. If we send her to The Ottoman empire, they'll take her as a harem slave. But given the unnatural "gift" she's attracted, we will find ourselves in a war. There are better reasons to fight a war than banishing unnatural beings from our lands," said Vlad the Impaler.

"I have a better proposition, Your Majesty," said Gabriel, attracting all eyes on him. "To save the castle from the unnatural being's threat, I will marry Princess Petra."

CHAPTER 20

A surge of gasps, including mine, emerged from the shock of Gabriel's words. Boyar Dobre almost got up and left, but his cowardice held him back.

"He doesn't understand what he's saying, Your Majesty. He is but a young boy of twenty," said Gabriel's father.

"If there is a price to pay, I am willing to do so at Your Majesty's command," said Gabriel.

I was scared to speak out loud for fear of repercussions. I could only whisper in Gabriel's ear: "You don't have to do this."

He turned toward me, pierced me with his gaze, and for the first time in my life, I saw what Gabriel's resolute face looked like. Nothing could change his mind. At the same time, I didn't want to ruin an innocent man's life.

"Are your intentions honorable, young man?" asked Vlad the Impaler.

"Greatly so. I intend to marry this woman as soon as I receive your permission, Sire," said Gabriel.

"The head of the Stoica family must accept such a coalition. Gabriel is not solely responsible for the matter," Gabriel's father retorted.

"The House of Stoica must indeed conclude, but how

would the decision differ given the benefits of such a union? Not only will the unnatural being be banished from the castle, but we will also have a Hungarian-Wallachian alliance among our noblemen," said Vlad the Impaler.

While the men talked business, I stood like a Thanksgiving turkey witnessing helplessly how my fate was being decided. There was no way I could weasel myself out of this one.

"It will seal his fate, Your Majesty," said Gabriel's father.

"He is old enough to face the consequences. Milady, I expect my kindness to have favored you well. But now it is time to pay the Wallachian voivodeship back in the form of an alliance. Given your noble blood, it has been an honor for my people to welcome you on our lands, but you are still a hostage in my castle. Under my order, you are to be wed to this young man and remain a castle member until the end. Do you accept, Milady?" asked Vlad the Impaler.

After he asked the question, silence became so thick one could cut it with a knife. With all eyes on me, I felt immense pressure. On the one hand, if I were forced to choose a husband from the castle, Gabriel would be my safest bet. At the same time, I wasn't sure about my feelings for him. Did I feel attracted to him? Yes. Was there a place in my heart for something more? I wasn't sure. Plus, a marriage would delay my efforts to get home. But given that I had to pick between marriage with a man I found mildly attractive and death by execution due to being an enticer of unnatural beings, what was there to think? The choice was clear.

"I accept, Your Highness," I said and bowed.

Another wave of commotion commenced. A few sighed in relief, others applauded, Boyar Dobre left the Hall, and Gabriel leaned in to kiss my hand. On the other hand, I couldn't even comprehend what had happened. The entire debacle exhausted my body and brain to no end. I took a few steps to turn and leave, but my knees buckled, and I almost fell to the ground. Gabriel raised me to my feet, took me up in his arms, and carried me to my chamber.

I circled my arms around his neck, probably smothering him in the process, but he didn't say a word. He laid me on the bed, covered me up to my chin with the quilt, kissed me on the forehead, and said: "Sleep. It will make you feel better. I will see you tomorrow."

∞ ∞ ∞

The morning bustle outside my chamber woke me up. It was still dark due to the cloudy weather, and only a grey beam coming from the window illuminated the room. Sleep indeed made me feel better and replenished the energy I so direly needed. But I still couldn't open my eyes wide. A heavy feeling pressed on my chest. "What could it be? What happened yesterday? Oh no, I am to be married soon," I said, and dread engulfed me wholly. Maybe there was still something to be done to change the decision. I had to talk to Mama Nica. With rapid motion, I moved the heavy quilt to the side and noticed wool socks on my feet. "*Who put those on me?*" I rolled off the bed but stumbled and found myself facing something. No, wait, someone. "Gabriel?" I whispered, hoping I hadn't woken him up, but I was unsuccessful.

He opened his big, dark brown eyes and smiled. "Milady, are you feeling better?"

"Yes, much better," I said as I tried to wiggle myself from the sandwich made by the bed and his frame. He placed a heavy arm on mine and asked: "Was your sleep unperturbed?"

"Indeed so." I shifted from his half embrace and rose from the floor to put some distance between us. "How come you were allowed to sleep in my chamber?"

"I wasn't allowed. I came in late last night. Mama Nica gave me the key," he said, presenting me with the rusty tool of betrayal. As always, Mama Nica sided with the handsome enemy.

"What if your father found out?"

"You are my betrothed, and I was here not out of ill intentions. There was still a risk for the unnatural being to return. My father will have to step aside on this one." He walked closer to me.

Before, he couldn't stand up to his father quoting family values, but now he's a rebel. Great. Just what I needed. An already attractive man to sacrifice his livelihood for me. "*Try going home now, Petra.*"

"Gabriel, I must speak openly," I said.

"I would appreciate that very much." He smiled.

"As much as I'm grateful you stood up for me and took such a major step as marriage to protect me. I, sadly, cannot do so."

His entire demeanor changed, and a new awkwardness descended between us. "How so?"

"As you well know, I am not from the Wallachian lands. I come from far, far away."

"Yes, from the Hungarian kingdom."

"Yes, but a bit further than that. And there will come a time when I must return home. I do not want to sow empty hopes and break your heart in the meantime."

"As much as I appreciate you caring for my heart, it is not the only reason I chose to marry you. Even if you return to your land, Zburătorul will follow," he said in a somber tone.

"Indeed so," I muttered. Was it possible for Zburătorul to travel through time?

Gabriel continued, "if returning home is a matter of high importance, I could escort you to your homeland not as a stranger but as your husband."

Wouldn't that be great? But no. I didn't know how to transport myself back. Much less Gabriel. Plus, how was I supposed to explain to him I came from the future. If other people heard about it, they would have a cushiony bonfire prepared for me in a jiffy.

"It's much more complicated than simply traveling home. As much as I wished to divulge more at the moment, it would make the situation far more difficult than it already is. But one thing I know for sure is that you are not a stranger to me. I haven't even begun thanking you for saving me from that creature," I said as I walked closer to the bed frame. He remained in the same spot.

"My only regret is I hadn't arrived sooner," he said and paused. "You have always been enveloped in a cloak of mystery. But it is how life in these times has always been. I am willing to accept that. My only wish is for you not to be part of The Other Realm. The world of unnatural beings is not where I wish to live, but once one is touched by magic, it is forever in their blood."

"No, I do not come from The Other Realm. The only unnatural being to ever touch me was Zburătorul."

"His touch wasn't strong enough to take you to the other side, for he was once human," he said. "Then I see no issue to continue with the wedding."

As a final attempt to persuade him not to follow through with the wedding, I rushed to say: "I won't be able to gift you my heart."

A surprised silence followed. He then began walking slowly toward me. "Is it a question of marital duty? Do not fret, Milady, you have my word, I will not touch you until–"

"*That is the least of my problems*," I thought.

He froze with a stunned expression on his face. One corner of his mouth lifted, and right when the sun rays peeked through the mosaic window in the back, it illuminated one of the most radiant smiles I had ever seen. His beauty transcended beyond any supernatural creature to ever exist and more than half a Century of men that are yet to exist.

"I said that out loud, didn't I?" I whispered, slowly transforming into a boiled lobster of embarrassment.

He didn't reply. He simply sprinted toward me, hugged me tight, and spun me around the room. After several rotations, he threw us on the bed with me on top of him. Our worlds narrowed to a bonded gaze that spoke about everything but in silence. For a second, I felt shy again, but he didn't let it expand and kissed me with fervor. I never realized until now how much I missed his lips on mine. He began kissing my cheek and neck. He stopped and looked at my collarbone. "You have one of the most delicate collarbones I have ever seen," he said, caressing the area.

His words turned my cheeks aflame. Goodness, I became flustered by someone complimenting my bone structure. I was hopeless.

Gabriel began trailing kisses along my collarbone, which ignited another fire. This time inside me. The heat rose, even though the furnace was lit the previous night. He returned to my lips and kissed me voraciously, caressing my whole body. I wished to touch his body with the same freedom he did mine, but he wore a leather vest that resembled more of a test of logic than a piece of clothing. He grinned at my failing attempts, rolled us around so I lay beneath him, and began undoing the ties himself, all the while keeping our lips together. Besides the many qualities Gabriel possessed, he had to also be agile in bed. Of course. What else? Was he also a sorcerer? That had to be the reason because I couldn't get enough of his kisses. And I had never felt this way. Ever. "*Call the magic police. I have been bewitched.*"

As soon as his leather vest and shirt, as well as the silky top layer of my dress, left our bodies, a knock resounded at the door.

"Milady, it is breakfast time," Mama Nica shouted from the other side of the door.

We scrambled like two outlaws in the middle of an illegal act. Even if I could pull the dress back on me, he wouldn't have enough time to dress himself the same way and not cause suspicion. So he did what lovers do since forever. He sneaked under the bed while I jumped back in bed and covered myself with the quilt.

"I heard noises coming from your chamber, Milady," said Mama Nica as she came in with a tray of bread, cheese, a chicken leg, oat porridge, and a cup of milk. This lady was determined to better my health by channeling her inner grandma and overfeed me.

When she entered, she paused and said: "What is this heavy smell? We must air the linen soon."

Apparently, my embarrassed lobster days were not over yet.

"What is wrong, dearie? You look red as a beet. Do you have a fever?"

"No, no, Mama Nica. I might need a bit of air soon. To refreshen."

She looked at me while I fanned my face to cool off, then she saw a second quilt lying on the floor. "I see," she said inconspicuously, but I could see the realization dawn on her. "Very well, I will let you have your breakfast. Make sure you leave when the girls come to air out the quilts," she said, accentuating the "s" at the end, and left the chamber.

CHAPTER 21

The news about our engagement spread across the castle like a wildfire in August. I had been accosted several times by Lady Codreanu and other noble women to confirm the news. While Gabriel's father had been avoiding me like the plague. Nevertheless, once the decision was made by the greatest authority in the castle, Lord Stoica didn't have a choice but to invite us for dinner at their home.

The Stoica household was located on the castle's outskirts, close to the village they ruled upon as boyars. Though they didn't possess as much land as Boyar Dobre, their family came from generations of nobles who fought alongside previous rulers. Since Lord Stoica was Vlad's second in command, the fighting expeditions and defense of the voivodeship amassed his great wealth. Thus, he and his wife, or better said, my future in-laws, lived a lavish and prosperous life even for medieval times.

At their house, we were greeted by a male servant who guided us to the main entrance of the manor, though I would assume Gabriel knew his way around his childhood home. For a modern eye, the house didn't impose much grandeur. But given the times and the deplorable state of the other houses around, the large two-story building, with wooden trims and a freshly done white stucco façade, resembled a bastion of state-of-the-art architecture.

At the entrance, his parents welcomed us solemnly. Lord Stoica wore a leather vest with studs and a white shirt underneath, as well as hemp pants and boots. His outfit paled in comparison with what Lady Stoica wore. She donned a long brown coat with fur throughout the edges and a red velvet dress underneath. She wore her hair in an intricate updo embellished with a string of pearls. If I didn't know who she was, I would've assumed she had to be the queen of a castle. As much as they wished to impose a somber demeanor, someone made their way between them, shoving them to the side.

"Brother!" A young boy not older than sixteen rushed to greet us.

"Marius, brother, I hardly recognize you," Gabriel said as he bear-hugged his brother. "You've grown taller than me."

"I wish, but I have a few more years to grow, and who knows, I might surpass you," Marius said with a wide smile resembling his brother's.

"Marius, end the drivel and guide our visitors to the table," said Lord Stoica.

"He's always like this when he's been gone for too long," Marius said to his brother.

"He probably forgot how it is to live with mother again," said Gabriel, and they laughed. "Let me introduce you to my betrothed. This is Princess Petra." Gabriel presented me to his brother. "And this is Marius, my vivacious brother. He's four years younger than me but has already caused more trouble to my parents than I had the entire time I lived here."

"It is not so, brother," Marius said. "You moved to the castle too soon. Otherwise, we would be in the same boat."

"That might be, my brother. That might be," Gabriel said and ruffled his hair.

"Come. Let's eat. Today, we have fish for dinner," Marius said and ran ahead.

I hadn't had fish since forever, as most of the time when they had fish at the castle, I was still a maid, and the closest thing to a fish I could eat was its bones. As we entered the spacious dining room, I noticed the expensive woolen rugs covering the walls while the furnace was adorned in the most exquisite tile. In the middle of the room stood a massive wooden table filled to the brim with plates of food and wine pitchers. There wasn't only fish on the table. There was also chicken, rabbit stew, and other meat dishes I couldn't figure out their provenience.

"Take a seat, Milady," Lady Stoica said. "You do not look like the noble kind seeing you so thin. Eat, please. We prepared the rooster just this morning."

Gabriel and I complied with her request. He sat next to his father, I sat next to him, and Marius next to me.

"How did the expedition to the Hungarian kingdom go?" asked Marius.

"Good, His Majesty garnered support from the king," said Gabriel.

"Marius, we are not here to talk politics," said Lady Stoica. "We are here to welcome a new family member, Princess Petra."

"That's not that interesting," said Marius and crossed his

arms.

"Marius," growled Lord Stoica. "I expect you to keep quiet if you wish to stay at the table." He didn't need to raise his voice, as only his tone made us all straighten our backs. The man could impose fear and respect with just a look or an inflection in his voice.

"So how did it come to be that the two of you got engaged?" asked Lady Stoica.

"It was a matter of castle security," said Gabriel.

"You don't say," said Lady Stoica, elongating her words.

"Indeed so," confirmed Lord Stoica. "His Majesty approved of the union."

She appraised me up and down as if trying to figure out something that wasn't spoken at the table. "So, if His Majesty approves a stray dog to live under our roof, we are to follow orders blindly?"

"Mother," interjected Gabriel. "Please restrain your words."

"Why should I? You're telling me that a servant of the castle turned out to be a Hungarian princess hiding from her vengeful family? What else are you going to come up with? That the moon is made of cheese?"

"Who said she was any good at being a servant?" Gabriel said.

I wanted to kick him in the shins, but my blue blood, or better said, newly tinted blue blood, didn't let me. But the surprise on Lady Stoica's face told me he had made the right choice with his words.

"And rightly so, a princess would never stoop so low as to scrub floors and clean chamber pots. And how is it possible for a Hungarian royal bastard or spy to trespass into His Majesty's castle when it is renowned to be impenetrable? Maybe she used her charms to lure in men, including my son?"

She most likely heard about my demonstration at the castle, but pretended she didn't know in order to humiliate me. The woman didn't have a filter. "*Lady, as much as I didn't want to be here, I wasn't going to swallow every poisonous retort you send my way*," I thought.

"Something seems rather unusual about you, Milady. Why would Zburătorul risk being caught in His Majesty's castle? They're well known for choosing easier pray."

"Mother, I do not know what you are implying, but questioning the honor of a noblewoman can be considered treacherous," Gabriel said.

"She might not be noble, Gabriel."

"Mother!" Gabriel almost rose from the table, but I tugged at his shirt to sit down.

"Lady Stoica," I said, "I understand that my less than grand introduction to the castle could deter anyone from a formidable impression. But I assure you my roots should be more than satisfactory for your family. More so, I feel like I am the one who will raise the status of my betrothed and his household. And let's not forget that I was given a choice to grant my hand to Gabriel and not the other way around. But given my lack of dowery, I see how this union could serve both sides. I could lend my royal name to your family's fortune while you could help me detract assailants greedy to muddle my noble status."

Shades of purple spread across Lady Stoica's face. "I demand a reading," she said between her teeth.

"A what?" I interjected.

"A reading. I have someone who will tell us who you truly are," said Lady Stoica.

"Mother, no one will have a reading," said Gabriel.

"Well then, I am against this marriage," said Lady Stoica and crossed her arms.

Silence hit everyone at the same time. If a marriage didn't receive a blessing from both parents, there could be no wedding, especially of such high status. But then Vlad the Impaler's words would be discredited, which would land everyone in hot water.

"You are insulting a princess and His Majesty's order," Gabriel said.

"What are you afraid of?" Lady Stoica addressed me, ignoring her son. "If you are indeed who you speak you are, then there shouldn't be an issue."

Everyone looked at me for a reaction, while the mother-in-law from hell smirked with one arched brow as she leaned on her chair and folded her arms.

If I refused, there would always be a seed of doubt in my story, and if I tried to appease my bulldozer of a mother-in-law, the psychic might side with her, and that would be a guaranteed end. There could only be one way to go about it.

"I agree under one condition," I said.

The tension pushed through the walls as four pairs of eyes stared at me. "I wish to be there only with Gabriel."

"What?" Lady Stoica interjected.

"He is to become my lawful wedded husband soon, so he should be informed about whom he chooses to be married to. In any other circumstance, I would have you imprisoned for treachery." I stood up and prepared to leave. "But I wouldn't want to mar our future familial union."

She paused to think and said, "so be it. The truth will come out no matter what."

"Mother, we must leave for the castle as it will be dark soon," Gabriel said, eager to end the debacle before it turned into something more.

"What? That's it?" asked Marius, apparently ready for a blood bath at the Stoica dining table.

We exited the house, followed by Lord and Lady Stoica. Gabriel and I bid farewell to his parents, and we were ready to leave.

"I will send a messenger to let you know when we visit the seer. May God be with you." Lady Stoica said and kissed Gabriel's cheeks on both sides. Then she threw me a poisonous look, bowed, and said: "May the truth be with you."

Just my luck. I had to prove to my in-laws that I was dignified enough to marry a man I wasn't sure I wanted to have as a husband. I wasn't even sure if I wanted to marry in the first place. Seeing how misfortune followed me at every corner, I must've stepped on some angry spirit's tail.

The following week, we visited the nearby regions' main seer. Gabriel and I each rode our horses while the Stoica couple went in an open carriage, which created many obstacles in reaching the seer's house. As we reached the outskirts of the village, the muddy road resembled quicksand, trapping the wheels of the carriage every few feet. Only with the help of a few stray boys did the stranded nobles get to the destination.

The village's last hut stood out as the most well-kept

around, and it was there that Lady Stoica led us. I was told her name was Nadia, a white magic witch (a reason to not fear her, apparently) who could undo curses, heal illnesses, and help find fated mates, all at the price of a coin. How convenient. As we entered, the stench of dead rats and hen heads tied to the ceiling attacked my nostrils. We were surrounded by a shrine of candles, crosses, flowers, and skulls. The four of us already seemed like a crowd in the tiny hut. Plus, Gabriel could barely keep his head up.

As I looked around, mesmerized by the décor, a woman in her fifties entered. She wore a dark robe with large sleeves, tied with a leather belt, and a dark hemp scarf on her head. Nadia, the seer, resembled a fancy witch who probably made more money than the nobles. She scrutinized each of us and stopped her gaze on me. Nadia saw straight through my skepticism. It was probably hard to hide it, given that I didn't believe in all this mumbo jumbo. Psychics were just as human as us, with the sole exception of them being a tad more astute in body language and basic human psychology. She invited us to a small wooden table covered with trinkets. For chairs, we only had filthy pillows. When she saw Lady Stoica, she quickly called one of the barefooted boys playing outside and whispered something to him. Half a minute later, the pillows got switched to cleaner ones.

The seer invited all of us to sit again. This time, Gabriel's mom approached the psychic, paid her, and explained it would only be Gabriel and me to receive the great "knowledge" today. The psychic smiled, took a seat on the other side of the table, and grabbed a deck of cards. She shuffled the cards for quite some time, taking a glimpse of my sour demeanor once in a while, then said: "For the questions you are willing to share with the world, you go to a priest. You come to me for the ones you want to keep hidden even from yourself. Whatever you try to hide is useless, as the truth always comes out."

"*That's where Lady Stoica got her philosophical knowledge.*" Apparently, my mother-in-law was a regular at the seer's hut. Gabriel looked listless. He didn't care much about what was happening, maybe because he had made up his mind, or maybe he didn't believe in it.

The psychic began burning stems of dried basil tied with a rope, hummed a few times, and then in a walk resembling more of a dance, she lit every candle spread around the room. All the while, she mumbled some sort of incantation that resembled more of a prayer rather than a spell. She then returned to her seat and mumbled something unintelligible.

"Even if some of you might not believe in the great powers of *Muma Pădurii*, it still flows through everyone's veins. She protects all life from evil spirits…"

"*No, she doesn't.*"

"She keeps the rivers clean."

"*I don't think so.*"

"She is the one who breathes in our air so we can breathe it out."

"*Don't get me started.*"

She took my hand, closed her eyes, and held it for a few minutes in absolute silence. My palm began sweating from the tight grip, but when I tried to remove it, she suddenly let go of my hand. The seer then took Gabriel's hand and held it for no more than a minute. After, the witch stared at him as if she saw a ghost. "It is you," she said to him in stupefaction.

CHAPTER 22

Gabriel didn't know how to respond. Even in the case of the psychic possessing actual supernatural abilities, I assumed I would be the main target. But she didn't give me time to feel lonely as she took my hand in her other palm. The move zapped us all as if a lightning bolt had struck us. We held back our hands from the pain and shock.

"So it's about both of you," she said and looked to the side in a blank stare as if solving math equations in her mind. She opened a tiny wooden box from the table, took something resembling an amber bead, and placed it in her mouth. By the way she chewed it looked like gum.

"What is that she's eating?" I whispered to Gabriel.

"It is an acacia chew. You can find it on the trunk of an acacia. It's sweet in taste," he said.

And I thought gum was somewhat of a modern invention. By now, her level of swag had increased exponentially. Where were the sunglasses when you needed them?

"Hmm, I'll need the book of incantations," she turned to a scraggly trunk and opened it. "I know you have one too." She looked at me. I froze and earned myself a raised eyebrow from Gabriel. She rummaged through the truck in a hurry, removing weird object after weird object: dried heads of snakes, lizard tails, large feathers, a handful of bead necklaces, and a crown. Where did she find a crown?

"Oh, this," she said as if she read my mind. "A prince once came to see me and didn't have any coins..." And then she went back to searching for the book.

Once Nadia found it, she placed it on the table. It was leather bound and ornated with buckles, a rare occurrence given that only nobles had access to leather. And for a second, I assumed the book might've been made by someone from the future.

"My grandfather makes fur coats. He made the covers for all my books," the seer said.

I began worrying she might indeed read my thoughts, so I asked, "do you read thoughts as well?"

She chuckled and said, "I wish. Every time someone new comes, they make the same faces as you, Milady. Thus, I assume they must dwell on the same questions."

She sat at the table and skimmed through the book for a specific page. When she did, I supposed the spell would be written in Latin or at least in some kind of words, but no, they were hieroglyphs. I could only distinguish geometric figures: circles, pentagons, stars, eyes, and flowers. If I didn't know this was a seer's book, I would've concluded it to be the scribbles of a teenage girl.

She began mumbling a new incantation, this time faster and with a more rhythmical beat. She pushed the book closer to us, still mumbling faster and faster and louder. She took my right hand more gently than before, as if touching a feather, but didn't hurry to take Gabriel's as if preparing mentally for it. After Nadia finished the verse, she stopped, exhaled deeply, and grabbed Gabriel's hand in a hurry. Then everything changed. A sense of agitation began spreading throughout the room. The candles began flickering, a circular gust of wind appeared above us, and all the animals outside began clattering. When the psychic threw her head back, I could take a closer look at the book and saw all the hieroglyphs moving, connecting, and disconnecting from one another. I looked at Gabriel, who shared my confusion. The chaos continued for several minutes, then everything stopped. The hieroglyphs returned to the previous place. The candles calmed down, and the seer's head returned to its original state. And all would've been dandy if not for her eyes which were rolled back. She stared at us only with white pupils.

"Until darkness descends, my tongue will speak...," a different voice spoke through her. It sounded much lower and with reverberation.

This time I was impressed. I never thought there were contact lenses in medieval times. Had to respect this lady's hustle.

"The moon and the sun have fallen in love," the voice said. Then it paused for the longest time.

Disconcerted, Gabriel and I glanced at one another.

"An impossible love. For when the sun rises, the moon disappears into the night. And when the moon shines brightly, the sun cannot witness it. An impossible love..." She then took another long pause. Then I noticed the black substance descending from her lids and slowly covering the whites of her pupils.

"Your journey was long," the seer said, raising my hand

from the table. “But yours will be longer.” She raised Gabriel’s hand close to mine. “The sun and the moon can be together only if the sun enters the world of night.” She placed one hand above the other, looked at us with her now black pupils, and said: “Predestined.”

She collapsed on the table as she said the word, only to recover the next minute. For a moment, the witch didn’t realize where she was and looked at us, confused. But then she saw where her book was opened, and her face changed to a serious demeanor.

“Whatever you just heard, forget about it, as your futures are not yet sealed. Thus, it might not happen. But one thing I know, lad, your bride here has been touched by magic. The Other Realm is waiting for her.”

The Other Realm? What in this con woman’s overblown imagination was that?

If Gabriel could somewhat explain the previous episode with trickery, this new information devastated him. He looked hurt to no end. It pained me to even glance at him.

“But I never met anyone before who was magical, except for Zburătorul. I don’t even understand what magic is,” I said.

My explanation didn’t matter. He was already convinced of my deceit.

“As you are not part of our lands, I will explain. Magic usually means evil,” she said.

“But you also do magic. Otherwise, candles wouldn’t be flickering, and the pictures on a parchment wouldn’t move,” I said.

The seer smiled and said, “I am but a bridge to the other side. Once you are there, you can never return.”

"But I didn't do anything to be touched by magic." I tried to defend myself once more.

"Magic touches those who wish it and those who have to." Every word she spoke felt like a blow to Gabriel.

"What does this mean?" I asked her.

"It means we cannot be together," he said with a decisive, somber tone.

I didn't feel any hatred or vengefulness from him, just disappointment. And that hurt more than anything. He took my hands in his, kissed them, and said, "forgive me."

"Forgive you?" I asked in disbelief.

"For I am not enough to be your fated one, though I so direly wish to be. My heart will ache for you with the pain of a thousand deaths and still hold you dear for the entirety of my life, even if your words deceived me."

"But I didn't deceive you," I said in despair.

He looked at me once more with a forlorn gaze, kissed me on the forehead, and left.

Desperate to fix this, I turned toward my accuser. "You keep saying magic here, magic there, but why haven't I seen any magic beings around except for that flying bastard who might be exceptionally good at tying ropes and be really into cosplay?"

"Cosplay?" she asked.

"Nevermind. Where's the magic? How can I not see it?"

"People and magic creatures live in different worlds and rarely meet."

"As in parallel worlds?"

"Zburătorul would've never crossed our ruler's palace if it weren't for you being touched by magic."

"But why did Gabriel react like this?"

"All magic is evil in the mind of the people. He believes you tricked him since you possess the power of magic. The witches' main spell is a love spell."

He thought I put a spell on him so he would love me. Pfft. The only magic power I had was to find and steal a necklace that put me into this crazy mess. And also, the ability to play the recorder. "What do I do now?" I asked.

"As I said before, your fate is not sealed yet," she said as she placed another medieval gum in her mouth. "But the time has come. You must choose, Milady. Your choice will not yet seal your fate, but it will decide your path. Are you willing to go after him and fulfill your destiny here or try to return to your lands on your own?"

My greatest wish since coming here was to go back to my parents, friends, and previous life. But now, a new need had emerged, one I never thought I would experience in such uncertain medieval times. I realized that losing him might hurt me more than not returning to my old life. His absence increased my feelings of loneliness I never realized I had. It pained me even to think about it. As much as I didn't wish to admit it, I realized I had feelings for him. No matter how much I fought with myself, how much I tried to convince myself, these feelings always resurfaced like a deep-rooted vine. And I had to do something about it now.

"I thank you, Lady Nadia, but I must leave now," I said.

She looked at me, stunned as if I had said a curse word. "May the powers of *Muma Pădurii* be with you," she said.

When I hurried outside, his parents were still convincing Gabriel not to leave, but he was already on his horse, and with one short tug of the reins, the horse galloped at full speed, fueled by the anger and disappointment of his master.

I rushed next to Lady and Lord Stoica and jumped on my horse.

"Where are you going?" asked Lady Stoica.

"Where Gabriel will lead me."

CHAPTER 23

Gabriel, of course, had to choose the most convoluted path to sway me from following him. He still didn't know one thing about me: if I wanted something, I would stop at nothing to get it. Or, in this case, get him. Plus, I already knew he would go to the part of the forest where he once took me. So his slick maneuvers didn't deter me from pursuing him.

When he slowed down a bit, I hurried my pace. As I galloped alongside him, I yelled, "please stop. I can explain."

He didn't even turn toward me.

"I didn't put a spell on you. You will understand when I explain," I said as he rode ahead.

Nothing. There was one last attempt at convincing him, but I had to try.

"I truly care about you. I love you," I pleaded.

Upon hearing my words, he stopped. Completely. I knew his horse-riding skills were phenomenal, but only after I was able to stop my horse much further than he could, did I truly admire his skills.

When I dismounted the horse, I looked around to find myself in a meadow surrounded by oak trees, and somewhere far away, I could hear the trickling sounds of a stream and the birds' chirps. No other animals in sight.

"Is this the same forest as last time?" I asked.

"Yes, but we're much deeper into it."

"Let's sit here so we can talk," I said, pointing at an old oak tree with heavy foliage. The weather had cooled the past few weeks. Somewhere in my time, people were celebrating Halloween and preparing for Christmas way too early while I was here counting the leaves falling with every gust of wind and declaring my love to a handsome knight. And I wouldn't have it any other way. The colors of green, yellow, and red entranced us, and for the longest time, we sat in silence, listening to nature's noises and admiring its beauty unhurriedly. After a while, the chilly weather got to me, and I began trembling. Gabriel noticed and wrapped his cloak around me, enveloping me in his warmth. He still smelled like the forest. What did this man do in his spare time? Bathe in pine branches? Still, even though I didn't wish to admit it but under his arm, I felt at home. The home I lost became his embrace. I saw he felt the same, but the question still hovered above us, and I had to remedy it. My only hope was for him to believe me.

"I told you before that my story is far more complicated than I could explain," I said.

He looked at me with hurt hidden in his eyes and nodded.

"But I never lied to you so I could have you. What I wanted was the opposite. I didn't want to burden you. As my story is far beyond your lands or the Hungarian kingdom."

"You said you were a Hungarian princess. Is that true?"

"Yes and no. I can write, read, and play an instrument. And given the privilege of my time, I could consider myself royalty in comparison."

"Privilege of your time?" He looked confused.

I sighed heavily, preparing myself for an explanation I wasn't sure would be credible. "I am not from your time, Gabriel," I said, looking straight into his eyes. "I come from the future. Many hundred years from now. It was an accident and—"

"From the future? Are you jesting?" he asked, dumbfounded, and I couldn't fault him for it. I sounded like a character from a cheesy sci-fi movie.

"I wish I could jest about such things, but the only magic I possess is being here with you while knowing what will happen hundreds of years from now."

"Are you a seer like Nadia?

"No, I am not, as I don't even know what will happen to me tomorrow. Much of it I read in books and only the major events. But what I know for sure is I care about you. I cared for you for some time now, even though I didn't wish to recognize it even to myself." I looked at him with determination.

His face changed, and a soft blush appeared, be it from the cold or he indeed felt shy. "You entranced me with a kiss," he said.

"What? But that's like the first time we went on a date," I said in disbelief.

"A date?"

"It's like when two people who like each other go somewhere to spend time together," I said.

"Then it was indeed a date." He smiled radiantly.

"But that's what I'm trying to tell you. If you already had feelings for me so soon, I already made you part of my problem. And I didn't want to involve you with this, for then my sole wish was to return home."

"Do you want to return home now?" he asked sweetly, puppy eyes and all.

His question made me hesitate with the answer. After all the events that happened recently, I wasn't sure anymore. "I don't know if it's possible anymore, and I guess it doesn't matter since I realized something earlier today. Even though the medieval era is one of the most uncertain times in history, I still wish to stay here with you and build a life together despite its unreliable outcome."

"I always felt uncertainty in your actions. You tethered on the edge between opening up and keeping to yourself. And given the fact that you were touched by magic, it made me doubt your true intentions. But from the beginning, I noticed something was different about you. Besides the way you speak and the way you move, there is a fearlessness I have come to admire. Plus, given the fact that few women or men can read, the idea of you being able to write, read, and play the pipe makes it more probable you are not from my time. Now, that I hear you speak so earnestly, do you truly wish to be my wife?" he asked.

"Yes, a thousand times yes," I said.

Gabriel stood up, grabbed me from my waist, and spun me around in complete exaltation. I hooked both arms around his neck, desperate to hold on to something. He took me into his arms and looked at me longingly. Then he sat us both next to the tree. His entire demeanor looked relieved as if all his questions and prayers were answered.

For the longest while, he stood motionless, simply watching me. Not uttering a word, just beholding me, witnessing the formation of something bigger than us. Something that would change our lives forever. Not because of Zburătorul or because he needed a wife sooner rather than later, but because we both wanted to be together from the bottoms of our hearts and the depths of our souls.

Gabriel contemplated me from top to bottom as if trying to confirm once more that I was indeed going to be his wife and lifelong mate. But after a couple more minutes, he launched himself at me and began devouring my lips. When our mouths met, the energy accumulated until now exploded, spreading charged shivers across my body. At the same time, he tasted sweet, as if biting into a ripe cherry dipped in honey. His kisses went deeper, igniting a fire able to devour us both. He then stopped the kiss and embraced me, fearful that maybe this was still a dream, an illusion, or a delusion. He needed to touch me to make sure I was real. He caressed my right wrist and moved his fingers across my arms, shoulders, neck, collarbone, and jaw. His fingers stopped at my temples when he gazed again into my eyes to confirm my love for him.

"I'm here. I'm real. And I will never leave you," I said.

"No, I will never leave you since I love you more than I could express in words," he replied, "and you will never be able to escape this." He began tickling me with dexterity. The man had too many talents to count. I burst into giggles. The giddiness I experienced in his embrace transcended anything I had ever experienced. He smiled as well, then rushed to leave pecks on my neck that felt like drops of honey. His hands caressed a trail from my shoulder and down to my fingers. He lifted my hands, kissed them, and pinned them to the tree on both sides of my body. Being encased between the tree trunk, him, and his two arms of steel at my temples, I knew no other bliss. He leaned closer. His face was just inches from mine. "You are the most stunning woman I have ever seen," he said.

I didn't care in what century anyone lived. If anyone heard such words from the person they loved, they were bound to become a wooey, gooey mush of happiness. I couldn't find a significant other my entire life, but once I fell through the cracks of time, I suddenly stumbled upon the love of my life. How was that even possible?

He placed little pecks of love across my forehead, cheeks, eyes, and nose. He then kissed me on the lips once more, deeper, hungrier, while his hands traveled up and down my body. Finally, we reached a level of intimacy where we were able to expose each other's most vulnerable sides. To linger in the trust we just granted one another. But I couldn't let him be the only one indulging in our newly formed bond. In excitement, I wrapped my hands and kissed him back, but then fear took over me. What if he didn't want a strong woman who could express herself more than was accepted in medieval society. He noticed my reticence, and I felt I needed to explain myself.

"As a woman of the future, I was gifted a sense of freedom by many strong-willed women who sacrificed their livelihood for future generations. If you are looking for a docile wife, I don't know if I'll be able to fit into that mold.

He smiled and released my arms. "A woman who knows what she wants and goes after what she wants is the wife I wish to have. I despise the unfairness of my time. The blind loyalty one must follow to survive in a world where betrayal lurks at every corner is not something I wish to accept. The rigid rules, the constant desire for power and blood, and the path already decided at birth are not the life I would ever choose. Just by being a firstborn male, I must bear my father's orders and continue his legacy by joining the army and fighting wars I don't want to fight. And the wars never cease to end. Once, we, Transylvania, Wallachia, and Moldova were a large, united nation called Dacia, led by Burebista. And even though we got conquered by the Roman emperor Traian, he brought prosperity to our people. But now we are three dismantled scraps of land at the mercy of our neighbors, The Hungarian king and The Ottoman sultan, who cannot wait to conquer us. I do not foresee a way we can keep the freedom of this land, even if His Majesty, Vlad Draculya, fights for it so courageously," he said. "But you probably already know how it will end."

"I fear saying what will happen in case my words change the future. We don't know what repercussion it could bring."

"I see." He paused, looking aimlessly into the woods. "I wish to live a different life without burdensome rules and constraints. I wish to travel. To see new worlds and the beauties they hold. Where things are different than here," Gabriel said.

"You would probably love the place I come from."

"Where do you live?"

"I live in a world not yet discovered called America."

"Astounding," he exclaimed. "Tell me more about your

time."

"Well, we have delicious stuff, like cake, and chocolate and, and coffee. And sometimes we drink hot cocoa and drive cars. And I just realized all my favorite things start with the letter 'c,'" I said, embarrassed by my excitement.

"I did not understand half of what you said, but I know all my favorites begin with the letter 'p,' like a princess, and Petra, and protect, and… passion," he said, wrapping his cloak around me once more.

"If we get married and have children, we should write them a letter telling our future generations to buy soda and technology stocks. My dad said our family would become millionaires if he had invested in these two."

"You never told me about your real family. What are they like?"

"My father and mother are very nice. My father is a car salesman, and during his spare time, he likes fishing and collecting coins. He always says he will find a coin that will make us rich. He worked hard as a Romanian immigrant to keep our family afloat. My mom is a kindergarten teacher and loves art, especially watercolor painting. Our entire house is filled with paintings of Mount Rainier. But I can't complain. My sister and I had a wonderful childhood. Well, until—"

"You have a sister?"

"I do. Her name is Elena. But she disappeared when I was around twelve during one of our European travels. My parents never recovered from it. For the longest time, I took care of them, went to school, and did homework all by myself. I didn't mind. I thought if I behaved like a good sister, she would return… Then reality struck, and I realized that it would never happen. But I still miss her so much," I said, trying to hide the shakiness in my voice. "Excuse me, I'm speaking in modern talk again. It must all sound like gibberish to you."

"Not quite. I like listening to anything you say. But I also understood the most important. You had a sister who cherished you to no end, and you did so in return. Even for a short time, it is a marvelous experience to have."

Indeed, even if I missed my sister greatly, I had to be grateful for our time together.

"What made you travel to Wallachia?" he asked.

"There was a guy."

"A man you wished to marry?"

"His name was Elijah, and we didn't get that far in our relationship. He tried to force himself on me, as a form of defiance and self-care I decided to travel to Wallachia or, as we call it, Romania," I said, trying to hide the sadness in my voice.

"The vile bastard. If I were to encounter him, he would've had to fight me and die an honorable death by my sword." His fist trembled in wrath.

"No, no. Duels were long prohibited before my time. And there is no way you could ever meet him."

"It is probably best for his livelihood. But do not fret, Milady. I will try my best to remove those dark memories. We can build new ones together," he said, kissing my hand.

It felt like peace was restored. With our hands intertwined, we laid back on the tree trunk, caressed by a slow swoosh of the wind. The dry leaves had covered our tracks, creating a canopy of warm colors. Only nature could make goodbyes so amazing. Silence became our friend again.

After some time, Gabriel asked the one question that seemed to be gnawing at him, "after hearing all about your life, I must ask again, are you willing to renounce the riches of your time to live here with me?"

"It has been decided the moment you left the seer's hut, and I ran like a crazy woman after you," I laughed at the description I never thought I would give myself.

"Hut?" he asked, confused.

"Like a house."

"I see."

"You know why the *strigoi* got kicked out of the house?"

He looked at me dumbfounded.

"Because he was a pain in the neck," I said and cackled.

"I do not understand."

"It's fine. I've kept this one in for so long that I desperately needed to say it. But don't worry. We'll work on the fine art of *punology* in time. I hope we'll have plenty of that, given I possess some seer knowledge. Though I fear telling anyone—" I began rambling again.

"Come." He shifted to the side, rose from our little nest, and gave me a hand. "We must return, or else father will send a small army to search for us."

Refusing to move an inch, I crossed my arms, made a pouty mouth, and shook my head in protest. He held his laugh as much as he could, but, in the end, after seeing my reluctance, he grabbed my arm and, in one smooth movement, tossed me over his shoulder like a sack of potatoes. We were just talking about me being a brave woman who knew what she wanted, and now I was being carried on a man's back, similar to a bag of vegetables they had yet to taste. The life of a medieval knight's future wife was full of irony. A sack full of irony.

CHAPTER 24

Radiating happiness, we rode our horses to his parent's house. When we left the forest, Gabriel let me pass ahead to get through a narrow path. We both laughed and rejoiced in our love until I noticed a pole ahead. My smile quickly turned sour when I saw a couple of bodies decomposing on stakes. Vlad had already begun his purge. The smell and the weird position of their bodies unsettled me. I assumed many times I would end up on one of these, but seeing it with my own eyes made me want to turn back into the forest and stay there.

Further down the road, I saw a row of stakes. The skeletal remains of those people were sprawled on the ground with their ribcages still encircling the stake. It was so eerie I feared moving forward. Gabriel understood my distress and gave me his flask of water. I was grateful for the few drops which relaxed my tightened throat.

"These are thieves that continued stealing even after being warned. There is no place for such sinners in the voivodeship. His Majesty gave them a chance they refused to take. They stand here as a warning for others," said Gabriel.

A cognitive dissonance brewed in my brain. From one

side, human life was worth more than a few stolen goods, but in medieval Wallachia, honor served higher than any life. During such times, the same action was considered cruel and honorable at the same time.

As we got close to the village, everyone glared at us as if they knew what we were doing and where we were going.

"They're waiting for you," said a boy, mimicking how angry his parents were by using the shadows on his dirty face.

Now that I wholeheartedly decided to marry Gabriel, the fear of disappointing Gabriel's parents made my heart beat faster. Unconsciously, I rushed in the direction of their house. When I reached it, got off the horse, and peeked through the gates, I saw them sitting on the porch. The angry aura they exuded stopped me in my tracks. I preferred to wait for Gabriel before I confronted them. When Gabriel joined me, he dismounted his horse, gave the reins to a male servant, then did the same with mine. With furrowed brows, Lady Stoica got up and rushed toward us. I hid my head between my shoulder, waiting for a blow of some kind, but the fury passed next to me and slapped poor Gabriel on the back. His dad looked from the porch approvingly while I, for the longest time, didn't understand what had happened.

"How dare you run away from your betrothed like that?" Lady Stoica yelled.

What? Betrothed? Run away?

"You want to bring dishonor to our family by fleeing from your duties of marrying this lovely lady? And on top of that, a Hungarian princess. Do you have anything in that head of yours?" She pressed a finger on his temple.

"Luckily, the seer peered in the future and said the marriage with this veritable daughter of the Hungarian king is bound to happen."

Gabriel held back a laugh while trying to protect himself from his mother's pokes.

I straightened my back, emulating the royal status I completely forgot about for the past couple of hours.

"Mother, I took care of the issue. He made amends, apologized profusely, and said he would never do such a heinous act again," I said solemnly, knowing she didn't understand half the words I said.

"Oh, my lovely daughter," she said, smiling like a Cheshire cat. "I knew your noble blood would shine through any misunderstanding. My son can be a fool sometimes."

"Mother," Gabriel retorted, pretending his feelings were hurt.

"We must have the wedding as soon as possible so we don't embarrass ourselves even more. If the village hears about my son's cowardice that made him run away from his betrothed, God have mercy. We'll never outlive the shame," she said, half-weeping, hands raised to the sky.

"I have already accepted my duty as a husband," he said solemnly as his father approached us.

"It took you long enough," Lord Stoica said. "The honor of the house of Stoica is on your shoulders, son. Do not let us down."

"I'll speak to Father Lazar to set a date. We don't have much time till the holidays start," said Lady Stoica.

I wasn't sure what exactly the seer told them, but I felt forever indebted for giving us such a tremendous gift.

∞ ∞ ∞

The morning after our agreement, I went into the kitchen to visit Mama Nica and let her know about yesterday's events. To my surprise, Gabriel was already there discussing something with her. Interestingly, Gabriel and Mama Nica's rapport resembled more of a mother-and-son relationship than the one with his mother. Then again, who wouldn't want Mama Nica to be their mother?

"Yes, I would believe it to be the right way to go," she said.

"What would be the right way to go? I asked with reluctant curiosity.

"What a pleasant surprise, Milady," said Mama Nica.

Gabriel approached me and kissed my hand.

"We were discussing wedding matters, Milady," said Gabriel. "My mother is adamant about respecting our traditions, even if the bride is not Wallachian. I asked Mama Nica to help with a few. When Mother married my father, she wasn't from a family of boyars, so she cherishes these traditions in honor of her upbringing."

"What traditions?" I asked, worried it would be something extreme.

"Usually, the groom must visit the bride's house with a few suitors and an older man or woman who will speak in his name. If the father of the bride accepts the proposal, then the bride and groom will be considered engaged."

Great. In these times, I couldn't even say the words: yes, I'll marry you.

"And you want to ask Mama Nica to join your side?"

He laughed. "Not quite. You see, the woman must speak with the bride's father or another family member."

"Oh," I said, remembering my orphaned status. But before I could muster my conjuring questions, Gabriel continued, "I considered Mama Nica as a substitute as she seems closer to you than anybody else here."

Mama Nica peered at me, unsure of my reaction. I rushed to hug her, making her even more uncomfortable.

"Yes, I would love Mama Nica to be there as my mother," I said, feeling my eyes begin to water. "When will you come? Wait, don't I need a house for you to visit?"

"His Majesty had let us use the castle and visit your chamber for the procession," he said.

Gabriel had thought of everything. The strange feeling of someone taking care of me overwhelmed me. Was this how it was supposed to feel? As if enveloped in a heated blanket? By the time I recovered, the date, hour, and the number of people were decided.

The following week, Mama Nica, Anca, Lady Codreanu, a few more court ladies, and I were waiting for the suitors. I paced from side to side like a caged tiger, desperate to calm all the unpleasant thoughts forming in my mind. What if someone attacked them on the road? What if his mother changed her mind? What if I lost my voice? Wait, I didn't have to talk. Good, because performance anxiety was not my forte. When my teacher told me to break a leg during a school performance, I indeed broke a leg. After, I never stepped foot on a stage. Hiding behind stacks of history books was more my jam. And romance books in my free time where I didn't have to do anything but hide in a blanket with a cup of coffee in my hand and enjoy. Now I was to be married to a knight during medieval times, and he was supposed to arrive an hour earlier. The narrow, mosaic windows were useless unless we considered winged men with ill intentions. I couldn't wait for humanity to discover the magnificence of large and tall windows. I attempted to settle the brewing inner storm by opening the door and checking if they were coming.

"Stay," said Mama Nica. "Such agreements take the entire day, and they are not expected to be on time."

I sat on a wooden chair and began fretting on one spot. Then I heard the knock.

"Who is it?" Mama Nica.

"'Tis us, the suitors. We are here to ask for Milady Petra."

Mama Nica opened the door as I was dragged by Anca to the back of the room. A lady came in to look me up and said, "she is of marrying age, master." And the entire group entered. I could barely see Gabriel behind the wall of suitors.

"We're looking to marry this young fellow to your Milady. We have a son, and you have a daughter, and since we've known each other for a long time, we should not try an unknown road but the one well known," said the suitor, a man in his forties dressed in traditional attire of the best quality.

"I cannot give you an outright answer," said Mama Nica.

What? Wasn't this supposed to be Gabriel proposing to me?

"We'll have to talk with our kinsfolk. We'll meet again around town and fix a date."

"But—" I said in a stupor. Anca silenced me with her hand.

Mama Nica turned, giving me an explicit expression to shut my mouth, while Gabriel chuckled from afar. Then she got out of the room to walk them out.

Stunned was hardly an accurate description of how I felt. Was I duped under the pretense of a proposal? I doubted Gabriel would ever do that to me.

When Mama Nica returned, she approached me and said, "the engagement is on Saturday at our church."

"What about the 'we'll meet again around town?'" I asked.

She laughed. "That's tradition. Some wait longer, others don't. Gabriel sure isn't willing to wait." She looked at me knowingly while I transformed into a tomato.

The night before Saturday, I couldn't sleep. The thought of my parents and friends missing my wedding saddened me. I could only imagine my mom jumping out of excitement and my dad trying to hide his tears of joy while Mei would be the best maid of honor. But I couldn't complain. I had Mama Nica here, Anca, Teodora, Lia, and even Smaranda. And the man of my dreams, Gabriel. I guess you couldn't have it all. One thing I knew for sure, my sister would be so proud of me. I learned from her to never give up, and after her disappearance, I learned to also believe in myself. Though I wished I didn't have to learn it in such a cruel way.

I realized I had fallen asleep only when a knock at the door woke me up. Groggily, I opened the door. It was the girls.

"Are you not up yet?" asked Lia while attaching flowers

in her pigtails.

"You have a wedding to attend, Milady," said Anca smiling. "Your wedding."

"I didn't realize it was late," I said and returned to bed.

"I think she's in denial," said Teodora. She came over to my bed and removed the warm quilt completely, making me squirm and search for warmth anywhere I could. I found it in a pillow and covered myself with it.

"Milady, it is too late already. You do not wish to make your groom wait, and especially not your mother-in-law," Anca said.

At the sound of her words, I woke up instantly. "You are right. I must get ready." Where was coffee when I so direly needed it? How these people survived on water and milk, I couldn't comprehend.

"We brought the wedding dress and shoes Lady Stoica sent you," Anca said.

"And I brought the crown from Lady Codreanu," said Lia.

"And I gathered the last flowers I could find on the field," Teodora said and sneezed.

"Why are you always the one to gather flowers from the field?" I asked.

"They make me happy," said Teodora.

"Well, you girls make me happy," I said. "What about Smaranda? Will she be at the ceremony?"

"When she found out you were getting married, especially to a knight, she got very drunk," said Lia. "We haven't seen her ever since."

"I see. I hope she will return to her usual self after the wedding," I said.

Mama Nica entered the chamber holding the rugs she made for my dowery, but when she saw me in my nightgown, she almost lost her voice. Almost. "What are you doing here not dressed? The suitors will be here any minute," she yelled.

We scurried to get ready. I put on a freshly cleaned chemise, and Anca helped me put on the wedding dress. It was a silky white dress with beads and pearls sewn around the square neckline, the cuffs, and my waist. Lia braided my hair in the back and tied it with a ribbon. Teodora placed flowers in my braid and handed me a bouquet of field flowers tied with the same type of ribbon. Mama Nica helped me place the beaded crown to which she attached a white veil. I put on my new shoes and was ready in less than ten minutes. Being a medieval bride required less preparation time, but the heightened stress levels remained the same in any century. Right when I wanted to take a seat from the exhaustive makeover, another knock on the door followed.

"They're here," Lia yelped.

Three men, including Stan, the night guard, and Gabriel's brother, Marius, entered and asked to follow them to the groom. We did so, and in no time, I approached the church. Gabriel stood outside with his parents and Lord and Lady Codreanu. He wore a new leather vest with buckles, a crisp white shirt underneath, black leather pants, and boots. He looked ever so handsome.

His mother spoke to him about something to which he remained oblivious. When he saw me, he locked his gaze with mine until we were right in front of one another.

"You look like a goddess. I cannot wait to worship you

for the rest of my life."

CHAPTER 25

Lady Stoica and Lady Codreanu came closer to admire my dress while Gabriel was taken by their male counterparts to discuss politics. Given the Wallachian tradition, we were supposed to pick godparents for the wedding ceremony. I went with those who knew me the least and did us less harm. Thus, after today, I would end up not with one but two sets of Wallachian parents.

"Milady," said Lady Codreanu, "what a marvelous bride you make. I remember the time when I got married. Lord Codreanu would listen to every word I uttered as if pearls came out of my mouth. Now he cares only about our estate, alliances, and war." She reminisced for a second and then continued, "but enough about me. Are you staying at the castle after the wedding?"

Before I could answer, the royal priest appeared in front of the arched door frame of the wooden church. "Ah, here is the couple," said Father Lazar, looking at me with an inquisitive eyebrow. "And this is the future bride. I must say I have never seen you during Sunday services," said Father Lazar. Indeed, when I received the status of a princess, I was either sick from being kissed by the Flyer or fighting my future in-laws for a marriage that could save me from said shimmery man. But as a servant, he must've seen me tens of times at the morning and evening services. And, of course, he didn't dignify me to remember my face.

"As a maid of the castle, I have received a bread offering dipped in wine from your golden spoon many times, father," I said.

"Ah, yes. Now that I think about it, you were the one who always made strange faces when you received the holy anaphora. Yes, I remember well. And you also liked to faint a lot during my services," he said while stroking his long beard.

You had to hand it to Father Lazar. He knew how to expose all my faults to those whom I wished to make an impression on and, at the same time, increase my already developed anxiety ten folds.

"Why did you choose such a humble servant of God, my boy?" Father Lazar continued the dissection of my personality and status.

"Father, turns out she is a Hungarian princess seeking shelter from persecutors in our castle. His Majesty made her his guest of honor," said my future mother-in-law boastfully.

"Ah, indeed so?" said the priest in excitement while Gabriel and I giggled at the sudden change in his disposition. "What honor to be hosts for such a noble cause. Do you find the palace suitable to your needs, Milady?" Father Lazar asked as if not five minutes ago, he defined me as a humble servant of God.

"Quite well, Father," I said, trying to tame my sarcastic beast.

"I now remember you were the mute girl. I have never

heard you speak before. Such an unusual way of words you have. From where in Hungary are you?" asked Father Lazar.

"She's from the West part of Hungary," said Gabriel, confident that Father Lazar wouldn't know the difference.

"You don't say," said Father Lazar. "I have a brother who lives there—" Father Lazar said and took some time to remember.

Our breaths stopped, waiting for him to end his sentence.

"—but I never once visited him. The world is truly a large place."

We then sighed in a duet.

"If everyone is ready, please do come in," the priest said.

"Yes, Father," said Lady Stoica as she dragged her husband out of a conversation about weaponry.

The Stoica and Codreanu families entered first, then the girls, and, lastly, Mama Nica, who tried to hide her nervousness. When we were the only one left in front of the church, I wasn't sure what to do next, so I asked: "Do you go in first?"

"No, from now on, anywhere we go, we go together," Gabriel said and extended his hand. I smiled in response to his cheerful demeanor, let out an anxious sigh, gave him my hand, and walked into the church.

Inside, I noticed the stark contrast between the usual bustle of the morning services and the solemn quietude it emanated now. Its piety calmed my nerves a bit. I was glad that by Wallachian traditions, the wedding ceremony would be limited to the closest family members and friends. I would hate to trip on my dress in front of the entire castle. Nevertheless, just in case, we walked very slowly toward the wall of icons in front while being aware of the multiple pairs of eyes following us. Their incessant gaze unnerved me, and my hands began to shake. Gabriel didn't hesitate to react and placed his other hand on mine. I looked at him. His eyes promised me that everything would be okay. And I believed him.

The ceremony was nothing as I expected. The entire time, two people sang the most beautiful hymns while the priest spoke and sang intermittently. We were given large crowns to wear on top of the one I had. My right and his left hand were tied with a white ribbon, and at the end, we exchanged rings. Thus, in the eyes of the upper and lower dominions, we became husband and wife. Except, we didn't get to kiss. And I was bummed. Like, I understood why. Those were the rules. But I didn't care about any rules shmules, I wanted MY kiss.

As we walked toward the church doors, Gabriel noticed me pouting and asked: "What's wrong? Are you not happy to be married?"

"No, no, I am," I said. Then I whispered, hoping he wouldn't hear me, "I just didn't get my kiss."

His infectious laughter resounded across the entire church. "That is redeemable," he said.

"*He did hear me, darn it.*"

The moment we stepped out, he grabbed my hand and pulled a vanishing act on everyone. The last thing I heard before disappearing behind the church was Lady Stoica asking where the newlyweds were. Gabriel leaned me against the church wall, gazed at me with the most earnest looks, and softly grazed his lips on mine. "Was this what you wished for?" he asked.

"Something like that," I said, still recovering from the sweetness of his lips.

"Or maybe something like this?" he said and lunged for a deeper kiss. So deep I could barely take a breather.

"Does this satisfy your wish, my lovely wife?" he asked.

I didn't answer. I felt like we were the only ones on a cloud of bliss. I hugged him, grateful to have found a person who understood me, but also because I loved when he called me his lovely wife.

∞ ∞ ∞

The wedding reception was held at the castle. Vlad the Impaler gave permission to use the Great Hall but refused our invitation to attend the wedding. "The land needs their ruler at all times," he said. Mama Nica prepared so much food that she had to place plates on one another. She bossed the girls around till they sat at the table, famished and exhausted. I thanked and hugged them all, especially Mama Nica. Though she usually hated hugs, this time, she welcomed me with open arms. Smaranda and the Dobre couple were missing, but no one missed them. After a few hours and several goblets of wine, the musicians played a fast song, and all the men, including Gabriel and Marius, gathered in a circle, placed their hands on each other's shoulders, and danced a traditional dance. The whole event seemed surreal to me. More dreamlike than reality. Then suddenly, the musicians began a slow melody, and Gabriel approached me to ask me for a dance. I felt waves of heat rising to my face. I didn't dance, especially not in front of people. But Gabriel didn't have any of it. He brought me closer and bore his eyes into mine. As we danced (I followed his steps), he whispered, "you've made me the happiest man today. I love you more than anything in this world."

It could've been the wine speaking for him, but at the same time, I could see his sincerity emanating from his entire body. He truly meant it. Stunned, I tripped on my dress and almost fell to the ground. Luckily, he held my waist tight and decided to spin me around while the guests clapped excitedly.

By the time a light appeared through the windows, the wine goblets were spilled, the plates were broken, a few boyars snored on the table, and everyone agreed it was a darn good wedding celebration. When the feast was over, the dress and veil felt heavier by twenty pounds. Exhaustion crept around my eyelids, and I was ready to sleep. At the same time, fighting with my tiredness was the inside tremor of "tonight was going to be the night." It brewed in my mind like a whirlwind of emotions. I wondered how Gabriel coped with the anticipation of the upcoming event. When I turned around, nothing on his face denoted anguish or unsettling feelings. On the contrary, he beamed with happiness. Gabriel clearly wasn't the kind of guy who took many things close to his heart. Unlike me, he slid through situations rather than dwell on them.

We walked to my chamber, tailed by a few noble kids who teased us about it. Gabriel shooed them away, but the entire ordeal made me dread it even more. Nervousness and exhaustion were taking a toll on me. I felt like fainting.

Luckily, Gabriel was close. He swept me off my feet and carried me to my room. "It is tradition for the groom to carry his bride across the threshold of their house. Or, in our case, your chamber," he said, smiling. "In no time, our house in the village will be ready, and we will move there."

Inside my chamber, Gabriel placed me on the bed. After, he kneeled and removed my wedding shoes. They were so narrow I was surprised I didn't rub off a toe. I removed the crown with the veil attached to it and crashed on the bed.

Surprised by my behavior, Gabriel asked, "are you tired?"

"A bit, but I'm also nervous," I said, raising myself on my elbows.

"You know we don't have to do anything today, right?" he said, taking his boots off and sitting next to me.

"I do, but I also want to."

He laughed. "Then I'm going to be the tired one," he said as he collapsed on the bed with his arms sprawled above his head.

"What? No, no. I'M the one who's tired," I said and threw myself on the bed, mimicking his position.

When he saw my vulnerable state, he enveloped his arms around my waist, rolled us across the entire bed, and stopped on top of me, pinning my arm above my head.

"Hey, this is not fair," I said with a pout.

"Raising your hands makes you open for anyone to attack. Better be your beloved husband."

"But you raised your hands first," I retorted.

"And you fell for it."

"Well, I'll never—" I wanted to say something, but his lips interfered with my ability to speak. And again, the same taste of honey and cherries invaded my sensations. Once tasted, one could never forget but also couldn't get enough. This was going to be a night to remember.

CHAPTER 26

Kiss after kiss, I could get lost in a sea of sensuality. A world beyond the here and there, similar to my experience of time traveling but so much more enjoyable. While one of his hands held my arms above, the other traveled across my body, waking up all of my senses. As usual, he smelled divine, of cedar wood and leather. If nothing else, his smell would forever remain embedded in my memory. He then proceeded to leave a trail of kisses alongside my neck, collarbone, shoulder, down my arm, and hand. He gave some love to each of my fingers before returning to my mouth. Gabriel released my other arm so he could grab the hem of my wedding dress and pull it over my head in one go. I was left only in my chemise. He then lowered the top part of my chemise to my hips and paused, letting his greedy eyes admire the bareness of my upper body. He began kissing my neck and collarbone, but this time, his trail didn't go on the natural path of my arm. Instead, he lowered himself toward the valley of my breasts. Kissing the bare parts as gently as possible.

"I don't think you realize how much I wished to hold you in my embrace," he said, kissing my breasts and lowering himself to my belly button. His kisses felt like butterflies landing on my skin. I was eager for the next one and the next one, over and over again. No way I would ever get enough. But at the same time, I didn't want to be a passive receiver, so I also began undressing him. To my dismay, the buckles of his leather vest made it frustratingly difficult to do so. Again. He took pity on me once more and guided my hands to where I was supposed to start. I succeeded, and with another swift removal of his white shirt, I could ogle at my husband's bare chest. I left my own trail of kisses from his neck to his chest, but he couldn't take it any longer. He removed my chemise, revealing my body completely. "You are breathtaking," he said, taking another moment to relish in the sight.

His words made me blush, and I tried to cover my most vulnerable parts.

"No," he said, taking my hands and placing them above my head once more, "let me cherish your body in its entirety. You are a goddess, and your body is the shrine where I must worship you. Those who didn't see it were blind."

His words mellowed my anxiety. I trusted him more than I trusted anyone ever before. Gabriel sat next to me. He released my hands, hooked an arm around my waist, and pulled me onto his lap in a straddling position. I wasn't sure what he intended to do, but only after the fact I realized he wanted easier access to my breasts. He began sucking on my nipples with such mastery it coerced an involuntary moan. My bewilderment granted him the satisfaction he had searched for, which he didn't hesitate to show me with a smirk. The cocky scoundrel.

He laid me on the bed and continued kissing my body

while removing his trousers and exposing his own nakedness so we could be equally vulnerable. He lay on top of me, shifting between my legs, embraced me, and went in for a deep kiss. At the same time, he began pushing inside me slowly but steadily, careful not to hurt me. His calm and determined demeanor dispersed every impediment of doubt I could have. The first thrust hurt the most. It took us several minutes of complete stillness to continue, during which he continued to leave sweet pecks on my skin. The second one felt more familiar with some pain along the way. The third time it didn't hurt, but a sense of foreignness still remained. He continued in a rhythmical gentleness, always assessing my face for discomfort. But I was too embarrassed to look at him, so I hugged him and listened to the steady thumps of his heart. After adjusting to the experience, something new began blooming inside me, something close to enjoyment. A new pulsating revelry that I had never experienced before. The passion grew like a scorching heat melding us into one. The deeper the thrusts, the deeper the desire.

If, at first, his touch felt soft as a petal, now it burned my skin. One thing I knew in this whirlwind of new sensations: I wanted more. I looked at Gabriel, who experienced similar cravings. His eyes pierced through me with need and wanton, ready to devour me. We rolled around on the bed several times. Sometimes, he was on top, delving deeper inside me while his tongue worshiped every nook and cranny of my body. Other times, I stood on top, caressing his chest with strands of my hair and dropping soft kisses on his chest as I moved in a suave rhythm. Being above let me have control over the intensity, bringing even more bliss in a world of never-before-felt sensuality. Just when I would feel more in control, Gabriel would switch us up, and I would find myself squirming in pleasure underneath him. The player in Gabriel liked to emerge at interesting times. Though I didn't dare complain. The same dance of entangled bodies continued for some time till something in Gabriel changed. He went feral and crazed in our shared senses. Engulfed by a new purpose, Gabriel pinned my hands above my head while he induced shivers down my spine with his slow, undulating moves of the hips. His thrusts intensified with the same speed as my moans. Our initial spark escalated into an electrical charge so strong it felt as if a live wire interlaced between us. It kept growing in intensity and spreading across my body in waves of pleasure over and over till it reached a climax I couldn't control anymore.

My mouth produced sounds I never knew I could make while my body trembled underneath him. I knew what it was called, but I wasn't sure I could describe it in words. Satisfied by my climax, Gabriel himself succumbed to the gods of pleasure. With erratic breaths and sweaty bodies, we found ourselves in a delirious dream of exaltation. It was bliss: the start, the dream, the afterglow. After he lay next to me, facing one another, we remained in a silent embrace for a long time. I wasn't exactly sure how it was supposed to be or feel, but it exceeded my expectations. In gratitude, I began leaving short kisses on his lips and cheeks.

"You know, kisses denoting completion can lead to new beginnings," he said with a mischievous smile.

I was too stunned to speak.

"But not today." Gabriel kissed me on the forehead. "It might hurt you, and there are many days ahead to relish in each other's caresses. Look," he said, pointing at the pillows next to us. "We were in such a hurry we didn't lay in bed the proper way." He moved my body so my head would lay on the pillows and covered me with the quilt. "Let me find you a night chemise. The firewood might be burning hot now, but mornings get quite cold."

As he went to get me a nightgown from the trunk in front of the bed, I remembered I had my knitted bag there.

"Could you bring the white bag, as well? It is hidden underneath all the linen."

He looked at me confused but didn't question my request. Gabriel dug deep, then a little deeper, and said: "Ah, I found it. What an unusual bag."

"It is my bag from the future," I said.

"You traveled with your belongings?"

"Yes, it was what I had on me when I traveled," I said as he handed me the bag.

I opened it, took out my folded white dress and sandals, and put them to the side. Then I dumped all the remaining stuff onto the bed. Gabriel couldn't contain his excitement. He first noticed the pocketknife. "What is this?" he asked.

"It is a pocketknife my dad gifted to me. It opens like this." I pressed a button, and the blade sprung open.

"Astounding," he said, "would be quite helpful in combat."

I gave him the knife, and he continued to play with it like a little boy. Then I opened my wallet and pulled a photo out. "This is a photograph of my family before Elena disappeared."

"What is a photograph?"

"It is like a painting but made by a machine."

"Fascinating. You have a wonderful family, and you resemble your sister so much," he said.

"I also have this." I showed him my phone.

"What is this? I've never seen such materials. Is this glass?" He knocked on the screen.

"It is. It is called a phone. It is one of the greatest innovations of my time. Unfortunately, it doesn't work now as it needs electricity."

"Electricity?"

"Long story. You just have to know that it is like an encyclopedia where you can learn about anything you wish to know, send messages, take pictures, and call people even if they're far away."

"What a wonderful world you live in." His face lightened with excitement.

"It is, but it doesn't cure all problems. You can have all this and still feel lonely."

"I would trade this glass brick to spend a life with you anytime," he said. "And I promise I will never make you feel lonely." He leaned over and kissed me.

Maybe he didn't realize it yet, but I was the one winning the lottery by marrying him.

CHAPTER 27

After our wedding, weeks have passed swiftly while we lived heart to heart, soul to soul with my beloved Gabriel. After a month of marriage, we moved to our house in the village. Never in a million years would I assume the house would be located right next to the Stoica manor, but here I was, neighbors with the in-laws. To my relief, Lady Stoica didn't bother us much, except for the incessant "when are you giving us heirs" question. And after some time, she didn't get the chance to see us as often when they were required to stay at the castle. Lord Stoica insisted she joins him from now on, and I wasn't sure if this was his personal need or a wedding present for us. Winter arrived, and many royal expeditions were postponed until spring. So even though the weather was cold and dreary, our love continued to blossom inside our little cottage. Gabriel took great pleasure in taking care of us, and I learned how to cook some traditional meals. We laughed during the day and made love during the night. And I knew of no other times as happy as these ones.

Mama Nica and Anca visited us several times. They explained some of the Wallachian winter traditions. At the same time, Marius became a regular in our house by helping Gabriel chop wood and building a shed for Vincenta van Goat. After an embarrassing amount of begging, Mama Nica let us take her. We also had a few new additions to our family: Henrietta, Eggatha Christie, Albert Eggstein, and their baby chicks. It took me a long time to explain these names to Gabriel. In the end, he simply accepted it as a quirk of mine without trying to understand.

During these times of mundane bliss, I didn't realize how winter rolled into spring, spring into summer, summer into fall, and so on for two years. Since these times were peaceful, Gabriel stayed home most of the time. That is until the spring of 1459. Once that winter's snow melted off the roads, His Majesty, Vlad Draculya had called upon Gabriel to return to his duties. I joined him at the castle. I missed Mama Nica and the girls so much. Plus, Gabriel had to go on another royal expedition. It was the first time in our marriage that he didn't sleep by my side for a month.

An entire month. No one had told me how hard the days of separation were. To stop my gnawing thoughts, I had to find something to do, but Mama Nica would shoo me away if she found out I spent time in her kitchen. So, I joined Lady Codreanu's sewing club, and, during the time he was away, I cross-stitched so many items, it would've been enough for three doweries. The hardest part was no one could tell me how soon they would arrive. It could've been tomorrow or in a week. The only thing Mama Nica said when I asked this question was, "before Easter, dearie." Easter was two weeks away. After several days, the weather warmed up, and I wished to enjoy it like the other ladies in the castle.

I decided to walk around it when dusk began settling its veil over the palace. The courtyard had a hilly area behind the castle, making it easier to admire the view of the blooming trees. Quietude spread across the land as most nobles had dinner at the time. I enjoyed the feeling of being alone, but I couldn't let myself feel lonely when I knew there was someone so special as Gabriel to care about me. Still, I couldn't deny I missed him. I missed his touch and his oh-so-radiant smile. I wondered if he felt the same way as I did. While in deep thought, the crack of a stick let me know I wasn't alone anymore. When I turned, I saw Gabriel. My heart leaped with happiness.

"Gabriel, you're home," I said, rushing to cut the distance between us.

"I hoped I could surprise you, but I couldn't contain my excitement and gave away my presence."

"I am quite surprised." I latched onto his embrace. "My only hope is for you to improve your agility. Otherwise, you'll never be able to steal some of Mama Nica's sweet dishes like I've heard you did since childhood. It seems you are getting old." His surprised look made me burst into laughter. Especially since he knew I was older than him.

"How did you know?"

"I convinced her to tell me everything about you over several goblets of wine. The woman couldn't stop spewing secrets."

"You jest," he said incredulously.

"Maybe. Maybe not."

"Then I must take measures of my own to find out the truth," he said and began tickling me, cutting my laugh short.

"No, I hate being tickled," I said, ripping myself from his hold.

"Do not fret. My fingers are stealthier than my walk. Come, let me show you," he said with a satisfied smile.

"No, I will retaliate," I said.

"Your retaliation will only bring me pleasure."

The man knew of no such notion as negotiation. And, in such cases, there could only be one answer: fleeing the scene. I ran as fast as possible, but the darn skirts impeded me from outrunning him. He swiftly reached me when I almost got to the Chindia Tower, hooked an arm around my waist, and pulled me tightly against his chest. "Aha, you are mine. Now, you must experience the wrath of my tickling fingers," he said and did so with no apprehension. Bouts of laughter resounded across the area, scaring a few birds from the comfort of their nests.

"Wait, I must tell you something. It's urgent," I said, trying to stall the next tickling session.

With a serious demeanor, he stopped and asked, "did something happen?"

I turned around once more, beholding his dark eyes resembling the night ocean. Though I was a good swimmer, I could easily drown in this ocean. I grabbed his face in my hands, kissed his lips softly, then brought his ear closer to my mouth and said, "you shouldn't strain yourself so much, you know, given your old age."

His curiosity turned to surprise and then to absolute vengeance.

I broke off from his embrace and went into the Chindia tower, hoping to hide on one of the floors. He didn't lose a second, getting closer much faster than I anticipated. I climbed the spiral staircase. By the tremble of the frame, I could feel him climbing as well. I wanted to show him I was a strong woman who could fend for herself, agile enough to outrun a perpetrator, and even in medieval times, I was no damsel in distress. That is till I stepped on the hem of my skirt and fell on my nose. I started to suspect the hidden meaning behind forcing women to wear skirts was to slow them down. I had a few more steps to reach the last floor, but no time was left. He grabbed me by my waist, climbed the last steps, and turned me around to face him mere inches from his lips. I felt drawn to his mouth like a bee to honey, but as I tried to kiss him. Gabriel leaned me on my back so low as if intending to drop me. I began pleading for mercy, but he ignored my words and planted an effervescent kiss on my lips. I drank in all his fervor, the need for me, the passion. I could never get enough.

After I don't know how much time, he brought me back into a standing position, giving me time to adjust from a dizzy spell. He went ahead and gave me a hand to walk out on the deck of the tower. I gave in, and we both walked out. We found three guards looking at us with surprise and then smiling at us knowingly.

"So, it was you who disturbed our duty," said one of the guards.

My cheeks turned aflame, a great reason to turn around and hide to save our lives. But to my surprise, Gabriel stayed, still embracing me. "My wife and I are enjoying each other's company. I'm sure you wouldn't mind," he said.

"I'm sure you can find another place for frolicking, given Milady here is an honored guest," said an older guard and winked.

"Indeed," Gabriel said. "I wish you a safe night." We turned around and fled as fast as we could.

Several boyars greeted us as we walked to our chamber and whispered something to Gabriel I couldn't understand. All of a sudden, Gabriel became serious.

"What's wrong?" I asked.

"Let's get inside, and we can talk."

Once in our chamber, I sat on the chair next to the table, and he sat on the trunk.

"It is about the boyars," Gabriel said.

"The boyars?"

"They are planning an uprising to dethrone His Majesty. He found out and is planning to punish those who betrayed him."

Was this the year when the Easter day massacre was supposed to happen? From what I've read, Vlad the Impaler wined and dined his traitorous boyars on Easter Sunday and then impaled them all on stakes.

"It will happen in a few days. You must leave the castle immediately and stay at our house."

"It will happen on Easter Sunday," I said.

"Indeed. How do you know?" Gabriel asked.

"I always knew about the boyar rebellion. I just forgot it was this year."

"Then you must tell me, is Vlad going to win?" he asked in trepidation.

"I fear divulging any more details, but I do not fear for you," I said.

"So, he will defeat his enemies," he said, smiling at the realization.

"Please fight as if you didn't know for His Majesty needs you at your best."

"Yes, Milady. You have my word of honor."

"Do you think His Majesty will impale all who betrayed him?" I asked.

"There is no doubt."

"Why does he choose such a terrible method of punishment? He could simply kill them with a sword. They die anyway."

"In a war where we are at a disadvantage, the only way to win is to become crueler than the enemy. Fear has nipped many fights in the bud." His face became somber.

I was surprised at how well he knew his ruler. Then another question popped up in my head. "What about the property of those who will be punished?"

"It will belong to His Majesty or be sold to merchants."

"Oh no, Boyar Dobre still has my pendant."

"Do not worry, Milady. First, we must get through Sunday, then we will find it."

"His Majesty's knights will not care about whose pendant it is. They will gather everything, and it will be lost forever," I said.

"Didn't you say you would stay with me here forever? The necklace is only a key to return to your time."

"We don't know its powers. It could be bad for me if it was lost."

"You forget I am also a knight. I will be there to find it. Trust me. Tomorrow, I will escort you home. And in a few days, you will return to receive your necklace. But before you go, please take this dagger. I'm sure no one will make an effort to enter our house during Easter Sunday, but just in case, keep it on you at all times."

I took the dagger with a brown, elongated handle with golden edges and placed it in my white bag. It was rather late, so we prepared for sleep, kissed, ruffled the bed sheets, and went to bed. But I couldn't sleep. Thoughts of the upcoming events kept me awake. I knew I should trust Gabriel, but I couldn't risk losing the pendant. The perverted boyar kept it to himself for way too long already.

Gabriel wouldn't even notice me entering his chamber. Everyone would be at the Easter Day celebration feast. I knew the castle like the back of my hand. I would be in and out while they ate, still safe from the horrible events planned for later. And Gabriel wouldn't even have to know. If he asked where I got it from, I could tell him Anca gave it to me.

It was now or never.

CHAPTER 28

On Sunday, I woke up at dawn. I put on one of my most comfortable dresses, tied the dagger to my thigh, tied a small leather bag to a belt around my waist, and rode my horse up to the castle. An eerie silence encompassed the premise. I tied my horse before the bridge and walked up to the gates. Stan was still there and let me in, though reluctantly.

"Did Gabriel tell you about today?" Stan asked.

"Yes, but I'm here for a short time to pick up something," I said.

"You may go but be fast. We don't want any women or children here in the afternoon."

I rushed to the castle entrance when I saw Smaranda coming out with a plate of fried chicken in her hand. "What's the hurry, Milady?" she asked with sarcasm.

"Good to see you, Smaranda. Hope everything is well."

She didn't dignify me with an answer and simply left. I didn't have time to think about her passive-aggressive behavior. Much more terrible stuff was about to happen. I ran next to the Great Hall and heard multiple voices laughing and having a good time. "*I still have time.*" When I reached Boyar Dobre's chamber, I feared it might be locked. And it was. My only hope was to try opening the door with the key from Gabriel and I's chamber. To my relief, it worked. As much as they tried to protect the castle, some things lacked common sense, like making the same locks for each door.

When I entered Boyar Dobre's chamber, everything looked exactly as the last time I'd been here. Given the room's layout, there could only be a few hiding spots. I searched underneath the bed and in his linen chest. Nothing. The last place it could be was his writing desk. The new ink pot had an intricate squarish holder made of silver. When I removed the ink pot, I realized it was a small jewelry box. Hopeful, I opened the lid, but there was still nothing. "Where could it be?" I said.

"So now you're a thief, wench?" a well-known voice spoke.

I turned around, and it was, indeed, Boyar Dobre.

"How did you know I was here?" I asked in a stupor.

"A little birdy told me so. She is one of your maid friends. She knows her place well, and you should follow suit instead of pretending to be one of us."

"I came to take what is rightfully mine," I said, trying to impose myself as superior to him.

He cackled and said, "you dare say I am the thief?"

"If it squeaks like a thief, then it's a thief," I said.

At the sound of my words, his rage grew exponentially. He shoved his hand in his vest pocket and took out the piece I fought so hard to retrieve, MY pendant. "Is this what you're looking for?"

I lunged at it, desperate to hold it once more in my hand. But he was too fast and moved to the side. I tried again to no avail. I looked like a small child trying to get ahold of a piece of candy. The boyar got tired of my attempts and shoved me so hard I fell to the floor.

He turned to grab something, unconcerned I could attack him. I took my dagger from under my dress and sprung onto my feet, ready to stab him. Eager to end this ordeal once and for all, I prepared to plunge the dagger into him. But, to my dismay, I couldn't. I tried again but to no avail. It felt like I was striking a wall that stopped me from pushing further. And if things weren't bad enough, Boyar Dobre began turning around.

"I know why you so eagerly wish to have this pendant as if your little husband cannot gift you more. You are a witch," he said as he turned to me. It enraged him when he saw me holding a dagger and realized I had tried to kill him. "You will regret this, wench," he said and struck my face, forcing me to drop the dagger. Distraught but not surprised by his violence, I sought a way out of his chamber. But he grabbed me by my sleeve, dragged me back, and threw me on the floor again. He unsheathed his sword, and for a second, I believed he would plunge it into me, but I only felt heavy blows all over my legs, back, and head. I curled into a fetal position and tried to cover my head and stomach. His wrath seemed to dissipate when he heard my whimpers of agony. As a final blow, he grabbed me by my dress and punched me in the face, making my nose bleed.

"I do not have time for such foolery. I am to enjoy an Easter Sunday feast as an honored subject of His Majesty. You are simply a nuisance I needed to take care of for quite some time, but your blood stains do not deserve to land on my exquisite fur," he said with a menacing grin.

Even though the adrenaline pumping through my body still numbed some pain, I began feeling a piercing jab in my ribs and knees. He must've broken something and took great pleasure in doing so. He then showed me the pendant again, dangled it in my face, and said, "is this what you're looking for? You've destroyed my life, witch, because you couldn't get your little amulet back. But guess what? If I'm not going to have it, no one will have it." He placed the pendant on the floor, raised his sword high, and despite my arduous protests, he drove it straight into the stone. At first, it didn't budge, but a tiny crack began spreading across its surface. And I felt my soul leave my body. As if a breath I had never knew I had within me had materialized and disappeared within seconds. The dizziness, mixed with the pain, made me fall limp to the floor.

"What is it, little witch? Lost your powers?" he said with a demeaning tone. "Do not fret. It will soon be over for you." He walked closer to me and began kicking me again out of sheer entertainment, sending ripples of pain across my body. I felt like death was nearing, and the only thing my mind could do was drift away to an old memory. The time when Dad watched his fishing shows and always got inspired to go on his next trip to a nearby river. Mom would give herself a pep talk while still finessing the mountain peaks in her paintings. Elena was always searching for the next great adventure with her friends. That day she decided it was skateboarding. After much begging and promises to not be overbearing, she let me go with her. I felt so grown up next to the other boys sliding smoothly in the skatepark. Then at night, Elena would sneak some candy into our room and would tell me all about that one boy she liked. She would fall asleep soon, but I would look at the glow-in-the-dark stars we attached to the ceiling and wish upon a star to have at least half of the exciting life my sister had. "If only I could turn back time…Wait a minute. I am in the past, and the biggest perk of being from the future is knowing what will happen next," I thought.

I didn't know why I couldn't hurt Boyar Dobre, but I knew he had to be one of the scheming boyars who wanted to betray Vlad the Impaler. His days were numbered, and today was his last one. The one thing I needed to do was convince him not to kill me at the moment, for later will never come.

He paused the blows and went to grab his sword. As he hovered above, ready to stab me, I said, "Boyar Dobre, you have won."

The perverted boyar looked at me in confusion, dubious of my intentions.

I continued, "His Majesty and the other boyars are probably waiting for your honorable presence. No one knows I am here, and few go around this part of the castle uninvited. Thus, you can believe I am already dead. Prolonging my suffering would help me repent my wrongdoings and receive my punishment, still fully aware of my sins," I said, trying to speak through the throbs of pain.

"I do not know what you aim at, but it will not work on me. Still, I am indeed late to the feast, and if too many realize I've been missing, they might suspect your death to be my doing. I will tie you and silence you for now, and later I'll find a way to dispose of your body without being suspicious. Your sweet husband won't know a thing. And who knows? I might also help him find his way to hell soon." He tied my wrists and legs with belts and my mouth with a handkerchief. A resourceful brute. After, he opened the door to see if anyone was approaching, went out, and locked the door.

I lay in silence, scouring my brain for a way to get out of there, but the agony reached a tipping point, and I would find myself going in and out of consciousness. The only thing I could do was scream for help and hope someone would hear me. Even if Boyar Dobre tied the handkerchief on my mouth very tightly, I scrunched it, which allowed me to yell louder. "Gabriel. Gabriel, where are you? I need you," I said, but the sound coming out resembled more of a whisper. I dragged myself closer to the door, got as close to the crevice underneath the door as possible, and did what I never thought I would do. I asked for help. "Gabriel, if you can hear me, please help me. I need your help. Gabriel."

Those words were the last thing I remembered.

∞ ∞ ∞

When I opened my eyes, it was dark. "*Is this what hell looks like?*" I thought. The only thing clueing me I hadn't walked through the devil's gates was the light shining from the mosaic window in front. I was in my old chamber. I guess they had it ready for the next time I would get my energy drained or injured. Wait, wasn't I supposed to die from Boyar Dobre's sword? The last thing I remembered was screaming for help. Did someone hear me? I wanted to squeal with happiness, but the jabs of pain pinned me back to the bed. The ruffling noises my limited movements produced woke someone up. When I turned my head, it was Gabriel who, up until now, sat on the floor next to me, resting his head on the edge of the bed.

"Petra, my love. You are awake," Gabriel's voice sounded like it could illuminate the entire room.

"What happened?" I asked. My voice cracked for the lack of moisture.

He rose and went to fill up a cup of fresh water from a bucket nearby. After he gave it to me, he said, "the fire died down. I must start another one." He did so with great dexterity, as per usual. Then he lit a candle and placed it on the nightstand next to me. Gabriel then took my chin in his hand, inspected my face with a pained look, and after a seemingly never-ending pause, he said, "your face, fragile as a rosebud, has been crushed by cruel hands. Good thing I made sure those hands will never touch you again."

Boyar Dobre must've met his fate, as I assumed.

"Why did you return to the castle? Why didn't you listen to me?" he asked.

It broke my heart to hear the pain in his voice. "I didn't think anyone would know. I was supposed to go in and out. Everyone was at the feast."

"Enemies lurk where you least expect them. You should've learned that by now. What would've happened if he would've finished what he intended to do? His death, then, would not have been enough." Anger began rising in his tone.

"Please forgive me, Gabriel. I am used to doing things myself. My entire life, I had but few people I could trust.

My plan was never to go against your word," I said pleadingly.

"You do realize I could've lost you." His eyes welled up.

"No, I would never let that happen. I would've found a way to reach you," I said.

"You did. It was the first time I heard you calling me to help you," he said, laying his forehead in my hand.

"You heard me?" I couldn't contain my elation.

"Yes. I was sent to escort Boyar Dobre to the feast as it was getting rather late, and His Majesty has great disdain for such disrespect. Thus, I rushed to get him. When he saw me, I noticed a peculiar look in his eyes which made me suspicious. First, I escorted him to the Great Hall, but then I went back to his chamber, and it was then that I heard your pleadings. The horror I saw when I pulled the door out of its hinges could not be described in words. Even when I encountered death on the battlefield with my very own eyes, I didn't know so much fear."

"I bet you liked to hear me pleading." I tried to laugh it off, but the piercing pain in my ribcage cut it short.

"You do try to turn even the worst of things into positive outcomes," he said, breathing a sigh of relief.

"Hey, as long as I can crack a joke afterward, it might not be that bad."

"Crack a joke?"

"Nevermind. Modern talk slips sometimes. But what happened to Boyar Dobre?"

"He earned the tallest and most bejeweled stake out of all. Boyar Dobre was the one who organized the coup, and His Majesty wished to punish him personally. I did my duty and handed him to our ruler in a battered but intact state."

"What about Lady Dobre?"

"You have been sleeping for a few days, my dear. Many of the nobles you knew are not between us anymore. Some hang from a stake, some have long fled the castle. Lady Dobre must've done so along with the other wives of the traitorous boyars."

"Smaranda had seen me. She must've told Boyar Dobre. What had happened to her?"

"When Mama Nica helped me take care of your wounds, she said Smaranda was nowhere to be found. She disappeared on Easter Sunday."

"Smaranda must've realized the people she helped were traitors, and fearing for her life, she ran away. I guess all things have settled now. Except for my pendant. I never had a chance to get it."

"I have it here," Gabriel said and handed me the pendant I fiercely fought for. "Unfortunately, it's cracked."

As I took the jewel in my hands, I noticed the massive crack in the middle and the four fissures spread across the four-leaf clover. A shiver crossed my body.

"Milady, you are fading," he said, surprised.

"What do you mean?"

"For a moment, your body seemed to become transparent."

"I didn't realize it. I only feel weakness, but that could stem from my injuries."

"As much as I admire your bravery, we should visit the seer again. This manifestation could be tied to your travel in time, and only someone tied to magic could enlighten us.

Even if you are not yet ready to get out of bed, it might be too late if we delay it for too long. We will need to resort to the help of additional hands, but it must be done as soon as possible."

While I realized his noble intentions could lead us to uncover something we might not be ready to discover, given the circumstance, it could not be avoided.

"I agree. When do we leave?"

"Tomorrow at dawn."

CHAPTER 29

The road to seer Nadia pretty much resembled the same muddy one we had traveled through in the fall. Unfortunately, I couldn't ride a horse since any bump would shoot pangs of pain throughout my body. But also, Gabriel would not have it, even if I displayed great confidence in my ability to ride. Ultimately, we opted for a carriage and suffered the same fate as my in-laws. We got stuck in the mud. Luckily, the man was the best planner I've ever met (he would've thrived as a student at my university). Thus, upon Gabriel's request, Marius and Anca joined and helped us push the carriage out of its swampy trap.

To my dismay, my arms and legs became numb while riding in the carriage. I didn't want Gabriel to know, but once we got there, Gabriel witnessed for himself the limp state I was in. He didn't hesitate. He simply took me into his arms and carried me to the hut.

Once inside, we noticed the seer already sitting at the table, chewing on her medieval gum with cards and candles in her hands. Did she know we were coming?

"Did you, by chance, send a messenger telling her we were arriving today?" I asked.

"I believe not," said Gabriel. "It could've been my mother's doing."

"I was in no need of a messenger. I already knew you were coming," said Nadia. "Where is the stone?"

Gabriel and I looked at each other confused.

"The traveling one," she continued.

My jaw dropped. Gabriel then walked closer to Nadia, placed me on the pillow next to the table, and I handed her the pendant. Marius stayed outside just in case, while Anca remained close to the door frame. Gabriel sat next to me in front of Nadia.

"Ah, yes. Here it is, the Eye of the Dragon," the seer said. "I thought I would never see one in real life."

Now that she pointed it out, its size indeed resembled a larger animal than a cat. But a dragon? Did those exist?

"It is a tragedy it's cracked," Nadia continued.

"Boyar Dobre had a hand in it," I said.

"I believe he already had met his fate," she said.

"I tried to stab him in defense, but I couldn't. How is that possible?" I said, forcing myself to stand straight and not clue her in on my weakened physical state.

"Hmm, sweet angel. You are but a shadow in this world. Many things must happen for you to be here, but the most important one is for you to have an unsealed fate. He wasn't meant to die by your hand. His death had already been decided long before you arrived," the psychic said while placing cards on the table.

"How do people seal their fate?" I asked.

"Some feel a shiver when it happens, and others discover when death whisks them away."

"Is my fate sealed?" asked Gabriel.

"Hmm, not yet," she said with a knowing smile, still looking at the cards on the table. "But I can already smell it. It must be close."

"I still don't understand how this 'seal your fate thing' works," I said, a bit exasperated.

"Do not fret, Milady. I will give you answers. And don't hide your weakness. I know you cannot move your arms nor your legs." She got up and took her book of incantations.

I realized she needed to go through the same process of incantation, mumbling, candle flickering, and hieroglyph dancing. As she did so, her eyes turned white once more.

"Until darkness descends, my tongue will speak..." Nadia said in the same low voice as before. She took my numbed hand in hers and continued, "time is but a parchment writing its own history. Once written, it can never be erased. The written word is slow, the read word is fast." The black substance began oozing from her lids.

We didn't have much time, but I needed answers now.

"Why do I feel so weak?"

"You do not speak when the voice speaks," the voice retorted. "But if you wish to know, I will tell you. The Eye of the Dragon doesn't have enough magic to travel. You will die soon."

"No," Gabriel interjected.

My head began to spin, and I felt like fainting. Thankfully, I leaned onto Gabriel, who offered support with his body.

The voice continued, "you die here. You die in your time. You leave here. You live in your time. The Other Realm will guide you."

"If I find a way to return, is there a way to take Gabriel with me?" I asked.

The voice didn't say anything, and the black substance almost covered her pupils.

"Please, I beg you. Tell us," I said.

Silence again. And only when her eyes got covered in black, except for one speck of white, the voice said: "Predestined."

Yep, that answered everything. I felt so enlightened I could illuminate a whole neighborhood. But nothing more could be done. There wasn't much room to negotiate with other-worldly voices who possessed psychics for a living (or non-living).

After the ritual, she fell into a deep sleep for several minutes. We knew from before how draining these practices were, so we let her come to her sense when she felt ready. When she finally did, Nadia looked rejuvenated. Maybe this was the secret to eternal youth. If I were to bring the information in my time, half the population would walk around possessed by low, reverberating voices.

"My guidance ends here, for I am but a bridge between this world and The Other Realm. You must find *Muma Pădurii*," she said.

"*Muma Pădurii*?" I interjected. I thought *Muma Pădurii*, or Mother of the Forest, was a figment of her imagination, but it was an actual being?

"Indeed so. She lives in the Forest of Celestial Rites. She holds all the knowledge about The Other Realm. It would be best if you left soon, for you do not have much time before the stone's magical powers scatter through the cracks. But be warned, it is a dangerous place. May the power of *Muma Pădurii* be with you."

"How do we find the Forest of Celestial Rites?" I asked.

"Come," said Gabriel. "I know where to go. It is close to where we first went to the river."

CHAPTER 30

Despite my arduous reasonings, Gabriel refused to go to the Forest of the Celestial Rites until I took a day's rest.

"We must find *Muma Pădurii*. She will tell us if we can travel together," I said.

"First, we must find a way to send you back to your time," Gabriel said as he tucked me in bed.

"You mean to leave you here? I'd rather stay." I crossed my arms in defiance.

"Then you will die for sure. I'd rather you continue to live far away from me than die in my hands." He caressed my cheek.

"How will I live without you? My body might stay alive, but I will be dead inside."

"We will find a way," he said, trying to hide the pain in his voice. "You must rest. Otherwise, I won't have a reliable partner to travel with. We can't stop. We can only look ahead." He smiled.

He was right. I had to sleep, recover a bit, and then aim all my energy toward this goal.

After several days of rest, we commenced our journey at dawn. At first, the road through the forest didn't seem as treacherous as the psychic warned, but the further we trotted, the more we realized how deceiving the place was. Though I regained some of my energy, parts of my body remained numb. I relied on Gabriel to lead and guide the way to *Muma Pădurii*. He seated my numbed body in front of the saddle and took the reins in his hands while supporting me to stay upright. Behind us, Marius followed on his horse and Anca on hers. I felt assured to have them as our companions, especially in unexpected circumstances. When Gabriel went to Mama Nica to ask for help from any of the girls, all of them showed genuine desire to join in our journey. But Mama Nica said only one could go. And given that Lia was still young and unexperienced, and Teodora's allergies would not bode well in the forest, Anca remained as the best contender. Gabriel didn't need to ask Marius for help. He appeared at the castle at dawn without an invitation. Who knows how he found out?

If not for the heartbreaking reasons of pursuing this journey, I would've relished in the wonders of nature. The forest resembled everything I could imagine a fairytale would look like. Birds sang their impressive soprano solos, brooks trickled next to us in an ever-moving stream, and squirrels raised their tiny heads to assess the trespassers who made unusual noises along their path. The pine trees, ferns, and bushes felt welcoming initially, but the deeper we went, the denser the foliage became. The natural path narrowed, and tree branches leaned so much in front of us that it forced Gabriel to slash them with his sword. Anca kept turning her head back, fearing a beast might loom behind us. Suddenly, the horses stopped.

"What happened," she yelled, aiming her question at

Gabriel.

But we could not answer as thc beast Anca so greatly feared stood right in front of us. A large, scraggly boar ready to charge into us at full speed. Behind him stood what seemed like a gate made of intricately woven branches. Gabriel leaned me on the horse and said, "please hold tight. I must defeat the beast before we can move further."

Marius also jumped off the horse and said, "I will help you, brother."

They both walked ahead with swords unsheathed and ready for action. The boar couldn't wait to rip them apart. First, the beast struck Marius. His sword had flung several feet away. Then the beast turned toward Gabriel and charged at him with double the power. Being swifter on his feet, Gabriel moved to the side and stabbed it. The boar roared in pain, but the creature didn't bleed. He then stabbed it again, perplexed that the boar didn't stop in his track. But by that time, the boar had pushed Gabriel to the ground, crushing his body with its hooves and pricking him with its tusks. Relentless in his determination, Gabriel grabbed its ears and tried turning the boar to the side. At that moment, Marius stepped in and pierced the boar in the stomach. But the animal didn't stir.

"Stop," I screamed as I dismounted the horse and fell.

"No, Petra. The boar will kill you," he said with despair.

I crawled toward them amid their intense fight and said to the creature, "we are here to see *Muma Pădurii*. Let us go through."

The boar froze but didn't budge, still crushing Gabriel's chest. Anca jumped off the horse and helped me get up.

"Our greatest fears are often dispelled by a touch of reality," I said and extended my arm toward the animal.

"No, Petra," Gabriel yelled.

I still feared the animal might bite me, but only for a second since the moment I touched the creature, it disappeared.

Gabriel took a deep breath, and with a helping hand for his brother, he stood back up.

"How did you know he was made of magic?"

"Magical things rarely bleed," I said.

"Let's go. Another one might come our way," Anca said and walked me to the horse.

We reached the gates and tried to go through them, but the branches twisted deeper into one another. Gabriel, who still had adrenaline pumping through his body, sprinted toward the woven branches and began slashing them with force. But the moment the cut was made, the branches grew back faster. His frustration grew to an unrestrained state.

"Slashing them will make them grow. Unweave them slowly and make a small entrance enough to fit our bodies," I said.

"Marius, bring the ropes and let's tie in the horses. Anca, help Petra off the horse. We don't want her to fall again," Gabriel said with a mellower tone.

I saw how his irritation grew with each new thing he couldn't control. The fear of losing me made him hasty in his decisions, and I couldn't blame him. I knew very well how much he despised magic. Nevertheless, he sacrificed his beliefs and accepted to enter The Other Realm to find a way to send me back. It ripped my heart to pieces to see him suffer so much.

"We can't stop. We can only look ahead," I said, reminding him of his own words.

He looked at me, absorbing the love I was sending with my eyes, exhaled a long breath, and began unweaving the branches. Patiently, Gabriel undid each branch one by one, forming a small tunnel, then he asked Marius to go through it first.

"What do you see?" asked Gabriel.

"All safe. You can enter," Marius answered.

He then let Anca go next, took me in an embrace, raised me several inches off the ground, and walked us through the tunnel.

On the other side was an oasis of greenery, a meadow of fine grass resembling the lawn of the expensive houses in Seattle. Birds of various colors flew above. Deer and rabbits shared a meal. Foxes and wolves played catch around the trees. The forest animals enjoyed living in this heavenly habitat and didn't fear us at all. Once they saw us, they surrounded me and began sniffing and nudging me to follow them. After a few steps further into the meadow, a wooden cabin appeared. It seemed like it was always there, but we didn't see it before. All felt like a game of mirrors and shadows. Out of the cabin, an old lady with a grey woolen shawl wrapped around her shoulders emerged. "I see you've received my message," she said undulatingly. "Come inside. We have much to discuss."

GLOSSARY:

1. Boyar (BOY-ahr) - a Wallachian nobleman
2. Brașov (BRAH-shov) - city in modern Romania
3. "Magnus omnipotens stella cadens,
   Largire munus tuum super servum tuum
   Fata resignantur, mea numina celant
   Recludam librum temporis in quattuordecim
   centenis."

   "Great omnipotent falling star
   Bestow the gift upon your servant.
   My fate is unsealed, my powers hide within
   Unlock the book of time in fourteen fifty-six."
4. Muma Pădurii (MOO-ma puh-DOO-ree) - a mythological old woman who has magical powers.
5. Târgoviște (TUR-goh-vish-teh) - town in modern Romania.
6. Wallachia (Wuh-lay-kee-ah) - a medieval country located in modern Romania.
7. Zburător(ul) (zboo-RAH-tor-ool) - mythological creature with wings. He is depicted as a seducer of unmarried maidens.

AFTERWORD

Thank you, my radiant reader, for picking my book. I hope you enjoyed Petra and Gabriel's journey in finding a way to be together. The second book will bring answers, but also raise more questions. And let's not forget the shenanigans. So tune in. I'm excited to find out your opinion about the book. If you could share a review on Amazon or Goodreads, it would make a massive difference for me as an author.

See you soon between the pages of the next book,
Lara

ABOUT THE AUTHOR

Lara Bronson has always been a creative. First as a violinist, pianist, and teacher. And now, as a writer. Lara has published a literary fiction novel, "The Shackled Balloon," but now has chosen something fun and exciting, like Paranormal Romance. Her series "The Vampire Genesis Chronicles" is full of wit, love, and all the juicy stuff one would expect from a romance. Besides writing, Lara and her husband enjoy parenthood in all its glory with their twin boys.

THE VAMPIRE GENESIS CHRONICLES

Bitten by Time

Bitten by Magic

Bitten by Love

Bitten by Hope

Printed in Great Britain
by Amazon